Euripides and the Sophists

Euripides and the Sophists

Some Dramatic Treatments of Philosophical Ideas

D.J. Conacher

Duckworth

This impression 2003
First published in 1998 by
Gerald Duckworth & Co. Ltd.
61 Frith Street, London W1D 3JL
Tel: 020 7434 4242
Fax: 020 7434 4420
inquiries@duckworth-publishers.co.uk
www.ducknet.co.uk

A catalogue record for this book is available from the British Library

ISBN 0 7156 2816 X

An earlier version of parts of Chapter VI of this book appeared under the title '*Nomos* and *Physis* in Euripides' in *Celebratio* ed. J.P. Bews et al., Trent University, Peterborough, Canada, 1998.

Contents

I

Introduction

GENERAL PURPOSE AND PLAN

The title of this book, *Euripides and the Sophists*, is (as often with titles) slightly misleading. In the first place, I do not propose to discuss the numerous passages in Euripides which might seem to reflect Sophistic ideas. My purpose concerns Euripides more as a creative dramatist than as a philosophic thinker. It is to consider Euripides' development of a few leading ideas of the Sophists (and, occasionally, of their contemporaries) and his refashioning of these ideas in certain plays, into dramatic themes of his own.

There is also another rather different way in which my title may be misleading. These philosophic contemporaries of Euripides whom we know as 'Sophists' should not be regarded as forming a consistent school of thought like 'Platonists' or 'Marxists', though this misconception may sometimes have arisen. Thus, when I use the term 'Sophists', it should be understood as a sort of shorthand for a somewhat disparate group of intellectuals who do, however, have at least one defining feature in common, though even this defining feature did not in all cases distinguish their attitudes (social, intellectual and political) from those of their contemporaries.

The Sophists (at least as the term is used in the histories of western thought) were the first professional teachers of higher learning in Athens. The term *sophistês* might, of course, also be used of any earlier (and non-professional) teacher, whether poet or philosopher, and of any master of a particular craft. It may even have been used of anyone deemed to be 'too clever for his own good', as Kratos sneeringly uses it of Prometheus at Aeschylus (?), *Prometheus Bound* 62-3. In the writings of Xenophon and Plato, however, the term is used almost generically of any member of this new breed of professional teacher.[1] Such information as we have about the Sophists has, for the most part, come down to us in three ways: from 'fragments' – (alleged) ancient quotations from their teachings and lost works (the 'B section' of Diels-Kranz's pre-Socratic collection);[2] from accounts and summaries in various philosophical and doxographical collections (the 'A section' in Diels-Kranz); and (most extensively but in some ways least reliably) from the dramatic representations of various Sophists' views in Plato's dialogues.

It will be clear from the nature of these 'sources' that a certain caution is in order before making any general statements about the Sophists and their teachings. When we read Socrates' arguments with various Sophists in Plato's earlier dialogues, and study the neatly organized 'Sophistic fragments' in Diels-Kranz (vol. II, *Altere Sophistik*, pp. 252-416), we tend to see the Sophists as a much more homogeneous and easily identifiable group than they probably were, especially in terms of their ideas. Strictly speaking, the teaching of rhetoric for pay (including, perhaps, the pragmatic approach to philosophy which this implied) was their only defining characteristic. They did not necessarily share all the same views, though there is evidence, as we shall see, that at least some of them shared some of the same views. So also, other contemporary thinkers who were not professional teachers may also have shared some of these views or discussed similar issues, especially on ethical and political matters.

These Sophists were, for the most part, itinerant wise men who congregated in Athens (from all over the Greek-speaking world) in the middle and latter part of the fifth century BC, when Athens was at the height of her political and economic power. We think of them primarily as teachers of rhetoric; it was in this capacity that they attracted wealthy young men as pupils, for in democratic Athens the art of persuasion was an essential means to power. However, Sophistic training and Sophistic ideas did, indeed, go considerably beyond what we would think of as 'rhetoric', or even as 'the political art', which Plato (at least in his *Protagoras*) represents as the Sophists' primary concern. Nevertheless, it was this pragmatic aspect of their teaching which determined that their thought in general should be centred on *man*, rather than on the cosmic speculations of their philosophical predecessors. It was this which led them to speculate on the origins of law and of civilization, and to reject traditional mythological explanations of such matters, except as symbols or analogies or unconscious reflections of underlying truth. Their interest in the nature of 'being' or 'reality' and in our understanding of it also started from man, rather than, as pure science might, in the external world. So, too, in the ethical thought of the Sophists, a certain relativity (with regard to individual men and their individual circumstances) tended to replace absolute ancestral values.

It will be clear, then, that the Sophists were very much in the *avant-garde* of thinkers of their day. So, too, was Euripides. From what we know from his plays, of his attitudes to politics, to society and to traditional beliefs, it is not surprising that he found much that was congenial in the approaches of the

Sophists. However, in inquiring about the use, if any, which Euripides made of Sophistic ideas, we are faced with what might appear to be an insuperable difficulty: our very limited knowledge, especially in any detail, *about* these ideas.

Owing to the skimpy tradition which I have described concerning Sophistic views and teaching, we often have only the leading idea, or the 'germ', of any given Sophist's thought, and so we do not know in any detail how he might have developed it. This limitation is not, however, as serious a handicap as it might seem to be for the sort of study to be attempted here. Euripides was not a philosopher, or even a systematic thinker; he was a dramatist, very much a man of the theatre. Thus we shall not be concerned, for the most part, with determining Euripides' own views of the Sophists' teachings or of the various subjects on which they lectured and conversed.

It is true Euripides was very much a part of the *Zeitgeist*; he would clearly be familiar with the leading Sophistic topics and doctrines, which would presumably have been a part of daily intellectual conversation in the Athens of his day. He may also, of course, have conversed with certain Sophists himself, and attended some of their lectures, but of this we have no real evidence. Later doxographers like to picture Euripides listening to the Sophist Prodicus (his younger contemporary), and to tell us of Protagoras actually composing, or reciting, one of his treatises at Euripides' house; such tales, of course, represent only the *kind* of association that seems possible between Euripides and the Sophists. Nevertheless, it is with Euripides' dramatic treatment of well-known Sophistic ideas and topics (Sophistic 'headlines', as it were, with which the theatre audience might be familiar) rather than with detailed Sophistic arguments that we shall be concerned. Sometimes, for example, we may find Sophistic ambiguities concerning traditional virtues reflected in the contrasting reactions of Chorus and characters to varying circumstances as they are presented in a Euripidean play. Sometimes what has seemed a simple Sophistic theme acquires a new complexity and a tragic meaning when viewed by the dramatist from a variety of dramatic perspectives. Sometimes, again, an outrageously novel Sophistic doctrine may be given an ironic twist in the elaborate parody of a Euripidean tragi-comedy. Thus, whether he treats his material tragically or ironically, this poetic magpie of ideas always succeeds in giving his thefts his own particular stamp. Fortunately, to appreciate such Euripidean treatments, detailed information (often no longer available) on the Sophistic teachings concerned, is usually unnecessary.

The same considerations apply to the poet's treatment of ideas which we label as Sophistic from their attribution to one Sophist or another in Plato's dialogues. The validity of such attributions (at least as they apply to detailed arguments) is, of course, questionable: the Sophists concerned are, at least in one sense, characters in the dialogues, and their arguments have to be recognized, at least to some degree, as contributions to the Platonic dialectic in which they play their part. We should also remember, in this connection, that Plato shows a certain prejudice against many Sophists, particularly when they are represented, usually to their disadvantage, as supporting certain views in arguments with the Platonic Socrates. Nevertheless, the major topics and specific doctrines attributed to the Sophists in these dialogues must have a certain validity for Plato's representations of their arguments with Socrates to have any point – particularly for contemporaries who might have been present at similar encounters.

While my concern in this study will be primarily with

Euripides' dramatic exploitation of ideas particularly associated with the Sophists, these and similar topics will also have been discussed by other contemporary intellectuals, such as Critias, known to have been an associate of the Sophists, and, of course, Socrates who, to judge from Plato's dialogues, was their frequent opponent in debate.[3] Euripides himself might not, perhaps, have distinguished very sharply between the ideas of the Sophists and those of Socrates. Undoubtedly, they shared an interest in various questions ('the teachability, or otherwise, of virtue', is a notable example), however much they may have disagreed in their answers to them; when such topics occur in Euripides' plays, the dramatist may well reflect, or even criticize, Socratic along with Sophistic views.

Euripides' treatments of various themes which he borrowed or 'lifted' from Sophistic teachings are of several kinds, varying from the tragic to the nearly satirical; thus it will be clear that such dramatic exploitation of these themes and teachings need not, in itself, imply acceptance or rejection of them on the poet's part. It will be sufficent for my purposes that the 'adaptations' chosen for consideration should bear the stamp of the dramatist's own creative originality.

Of the several Sophistic themes in which Euripides showed more than a passing interest, I have selected only five. I have also, in each case, limited my discussion of Euripidean treatments to two or three plays, and sometimes to only one, in which the dramatic point of the adaptations seem particularly clear.

Of the five topics chosen, the first two concern the question of the nature and teachability of 'virtue'; the third concerns the power (especially the political power) and the abuses of rhetoric; the fourth, the relativity of 'virtue'; the last, the significance of *nomos*, 'social law' or 'custom' in various contexts, particularly in confrontation with *phusis*, 'natural law'.

My procedure in the first two chapters (II and III) and in the last two (V and VI) will be to begin with an indication, consisting as far as possible of quotations of fragments and selections relevant to the Sophistic ideas and teachings concerned, and then to follow these with discussions of the relevant Euripidean plays and passages. In the intervening chapter (IV), on the power and abuses of rhetoric, my procedure will be slightly different. I shall try to indicate from two plays Euripides' exemplification of these two aspects of Sophistic rhetoric, especially in a political context. In one instance the dramatic presentation appears (as it does in some of the dramatizations of philosophic issues) to outdo the Sophists themselves – in this case in their own art of persuasion.

Inevitably, in these discussions, there will be occasional overlaps of material, particularly of Sophistic passages on one or another of the 'virtues'. On these occasions, it has seemed preferable to repeat a few brief quotations, or citations, rather than to ask readers to turn back to the page of their earlier occurrence.

SOME PREVIOUS VIEWS

As I have indicated above, many scholars have commented on various Euripidean passages which seem to reflect Sophistic ideas in one way or another. I mention now some examples of the relatively few scholars who have considered the matter in greater detail. Among critics of an earlier generation, Nestle and Decharme were particularly interested in the relation between Euripides and the philosophic and intellectual concerns of his time.[4] However, both these critics, perhaps in accordance with their own *Zeitgeist*, have failed to distinguish sufficiently sharply (and certainly insufficiently for the purposes of the present study) between Euripides the dramatist, and Euripides the thinker (as they have tended to regard him).

Thus, Nestle regards our poet as a serious seeker after truth in religious, ethical and political matters, eager to present his findings to his fellow-citizens through the medium of the theatre of Dionysus. (This was, perhaps, sometimes the case but not, in my opinion, consistently so.) Nestle remains ambiguous, however, about the actual influence of the Sophists on Euripides, which he discusses in several different contexts, and on their congeniality to the poet. Thus Nestle believes that Euripides shares with the Sophists their scepticism about the traditional gods and was interested, as they were, in the contrast between *phusis* and *nomos*, and also in the question whether the names of things (*onomata*) really represent the things (*chrêmata*) themselves. Likewise, in Nestle's view, Euripides also shared at least to a degree the Sophistic belief in ethical relativity introduced by Protagoras, though Nestle questions whether Euripides adopted as extreme a position as the Sophists did on this matter.[5] Here as elsewhere, Nestle does not, however, make sufficent allowance for dramatic flexibility or, in some cases, for the dramatic point involved, in considering the views expressed by various Euripidean characters. This is particularly true in his treatment of Sophistic rhetoric. Thus, of Polyneices' declaration (at *Phoenissae* 469ff.) about Eteocles' oratory, 'A just cause needs no artful turn of phrase!' Nestle comments, 'Euripides wants nothing to do with the false specious rhetoric (*unwahren Redekunst*) of the Sophists.'[6] This may well be true but Nestle makes little allowance, here or elsewhere, for the adaptation of various views to the dramatic character expressing them. Nevertheless, Nestle should certainly be consulted on various reflections of Sophistic views to be considered in the following chapters.

Decharme is considerably more concerned than is Nestle with distinguishing the opinions expressed by characters in Euripides' plays from those which he believes to be the poet's own. To this end he indicates three criteria.[7] One concerns the occurrence of certain opinions, their frequency and their re-appearance at different periods of the poet's career. Another concerns their appropriateness to the speaker and their relevance to the dramatic occasion. The third (the subtlest of the three) concerns dramatic 'mannerisms', alleged signposts by which the poet draws attention to an opinion. Not all readers, perhaps, will share Decharme's confidence in these criteria, but he does make an honest attempt to discern Euripides' own views on traditional religion, philosophy and social and political affairs.

Thus we see that Decharme is more interested in Euripides' views than in his dramatic exploitation of those of the Sophists. Moreover, what discussion there is of Euripides' interaction with Sophistic teachings[8] is limited to a few Euripidean passages allegedly reflecting Protagoras' subjectivism, or illustratng Sophistic skills in the defence of unjust causes. Even here, however, Decharme quotes other passages to suggest that the poet was critical of such uses of Sophistic rhetoric: in these various examples, Decharme, like Nestle, seems to pay too little heed to the dramatic context and purpose of the passages cited.

Decharme's general conclusion is that Euripides, though showing a real kinship with the Sophistic spirit, was already too mature by the time that he may have associated with any Sophists for them to have had much effect on his thinking.[9] However, this critic also suggests that 'had [he] not given up philosophy for the stage, [Euripides] might possibly have become, without the aid of anybody's instruction, ... one of the greatest, if not the first, among the sophists.'[10]

Untersteiner is still another critic of an earlier generation who tends to find a close philosophic relation between Euripides and the Sophists.[11] Indeed, this scholar seems to believe (sometimes on dubious evidence) in closer exchanges of ideas between the poet and the philosopher than do the other two critics just discussed. Consider, for example, his rather gullible acceptance of the biographical anecdote in Diogenes Laertius that Protagoras had read the beginning of his work 'On the Gods' at Euripides' house.[12] Moreover, Untersteiner's work is primarily about the Sophists and tends to refer to Euripides only at certain specific points.

Contemporary critics, particularly the more recent ones, have tended to see Euripides as very much a part of the Sophistic *Zeitgeist* of the second half of the fifth century. Unlike critics of an earlier generation, they have, with a few exceptions, recognized that he was a primarily a dramatist rather than a philosopher or a political thinker. One or two of these critics have also made the good point that Euripides often succeeded in expressing, in dramatic terms and to a wider audience than that enjoyed by professional teachers, Sophistic debates, particularly on controversial political matters. On this and related points see particularly the discussions by Croally, Goldhill and Vernant.[13] Thus there has, on the whole, been a tendency recently to regard Euripides not as primarily critical of the Sophists (as we have seen that Nestle sometimes suggested) but rather as their ally. Among contemporary studies (in addition to those just mentioned) which I have found most useful, are those of Burian, Buxton, Classen, Collard, Gregory, Lloyd and Michelini.[14] I hope it will become clear from the discussions in the following chapters how my own approach differs from one or another of these critics.

EURIPIDES AND SOME SOPHISTIC VIEWS OF THE GODS

This final section of my introductory chapter needs, perhaps, a preliminary word of explanation. Euripides' treatment of the gods and of traditional mythology has, of course, bulked large in many studies of the dramatist. Nevertheless, varied as Euripides' treatments of the gods in different plays may appear to be, they do, I think, have certain features in common which also show a clearly discernible relation to Sophistic teachings and to Euripidean attitudes, of one kind or another, toward them. That subject differs, in that it is both more wide-ranging and more nebulous, from the discussions in the following chapters, which concern Euripidean treatments of specific Sophistic themes. I shall content myself, therefore, with concluding this introduction by quoting and discussing a few Euripidean passages which exemplify, in a particularly striking way, certain typical features of Sophistic thought on 'the mythical tradition' and of Euripides' reactions to them.

There is a strange passage on the gods in Euripides' *Heracles* which seems to contradict the whole plot, or *muthos*, on which the play is based. When Heracles recovers from the madness induced by Hera in jealous rage against Heracles' father, Zeus, he declares to his friend Theseus:

> I, for my part, do not believe that the gods lust after adulterous liaisons, nor that they bind one another in chains. I don't think that this is true, nor will I ever

believe it, nor that one god is master over another. For god, if he is truly god, lacks nothing (*deitai* ... *oudenos*).
(*HF* 1341-6)

It has been made quite clear in the play that Heracles knows who has maddened him and why (1303-10). Yet in the midst of several passages excoriating Hera for her deed (one of which [1307-10] mentions Hera's motive, her jealousy over Zeus' adultery with Heracles' mother Alcmene) we read this extraordinary passage denying that the gods can ever be guilty of such offences.

A Sophistic fragment from Antiphon's essay on 'Truth' expresses a similar idea:

Wherefore he [the god?] needs nothing (*oudenos deitai*) and receives nothing from anyone, but is completely self-sufficent. (D-K 87 B10)

The subject of this statement is unspecified. Presumably it is *theos* ('god'), or possibly *nous*, the Anaxagorean 'world mind'. (The latter is the view of A. Diès, here quoted by Diels, who regards the fragment as a logical continuation of Antiphon B1, and both as a paraphrase of Anaxagoras.) However, several fragments of Xenophanes indicate that this view of the gods was held long before Antiphon and his fifth-century contemporaries, for in the sixth century Xenophanes had clearly criticized both Homer and Hesiod for attributing to the gods such shameful deeds as 'theft, adultery and deception of one another' (see D-K 21 B12 and B13) and had even postulated the self-sufficency and omniscience of one supreme god:

There is one god. The greatest among gods and men. [B23]

[God] is perfect in sight, hearing, and understanding. [B24]

[God] moves everything without effort by the thought of his mind. [B25]

It seems clear, then, that Euripides, in the passage quoted from *Heracles*, is reflecting a view of the gods which, if not original, was at least current in contemporary Sophistic thought. What, then, is Euripides' *dramatic* purpose in putting this Sophistic view in the mouth of Heracles? The theme of *Heracles* involves, *inter alia*, a contrast between the *philia* of human heroes, such as Heracles and Theseus, and the uncaring and immoral deeds of the traditional gods of myth. In order to express this theme, the dramatist has had to present the gods in their traditional anthropomorphic form. Now, at 1341-6, he raises the shutter, as it were, for a moment to let the audience share in a more explicit recognition of what the action of the play has expressed (by implication) in the mythical terms proper to this dramatic treatment, namely the unreality, the incredibility even, of this traditional view of the gods. In this play, then (to whose meaning this 'problem passage' is in some ways a key), Euripides provides a novel and creative expression of a contemporary philosophic view.[15]

In *Electra*, Euripides presents his version of the traditional legend of the vengeance of Electra and Orestes against Aegisthus and Clytemnestra, their mother, for the murder of their father Agamemnon. Just before Orestes departs to commit the first deed of vengeance (against Aegisthus), Euripides has the Chorus sing an ode which (like the preceding ode at vv. 432-86) has little to do with the action of this very realistic and (for a Greek Tragedy) secular play. This ode (the second stasimon, at 699-746) celebrates the myth of Thyestes' seduction of Atreus' wife in order to secure the golden lamb, symbol of kingship. The mythical digression ends with an account of how Zeus reversed the course of the sun in divine outrage at Thyestes' deed and with the observation that, if Clytemnestra had remembered such tales of divine punishment, she would never have dared to slay her husband (745-6).

> *Legetai* (so they say) [comments the Chorus, non-committally] but from me it wins little belief that Zeus would reverse the golden-visaged course of the sun, changing it to punish human wrong. But these cautionary tales *do* help to keep mortals in the service of the gods.
> (*El.* 737-44)

We find a similar, though somewhat more radical explanation of divine myths as of 'cautionary' origin, in a fragment from Critias' *Sisyphus*. The speaker is explaining the invention of the gods as a part of the evolution of civilized society. After retributive laws had been devised but men still continued to do unjust deeds in secret, then (in the opinion of the speaker):

> ... a certain wise man 'discovered' fear of the gods for mortals so that wicked men might be fearful if they did or said or thought anything [unjust]. (D-K 88 B25)

(It should be noted, however, that a few verses from this same fragment of Critias' *Sisyphus*, most of which develops material similar to that of the passage quoted above, have been attributed, by Aetius, to Euripides, who also wrote a satyr-play, *Sisyphus*.)

It seems likely, then, that in the Chorus' somewhat sceptical comment Euripides is letting the Chorus reflect a current Sophistic view of traditional myths about the gods, particularly with regard to divine punishments of human offences. Once again we may ask what the dramatist's intention is, in this passage, with regard to the play as a whole.

It is generally agreed that Electra's motivation for vengeance (particularly against Clytemnestra) is presented in more realistic and psychological terms than was traditionally the case. In Aeschylus' *Choephori* (*The Libation Bearers*), neither Orestes nor Electra (who plays a relatively minor role in the play) is represented as having much choice in fulfilling the god Apollo's command to take vengeance. In Euripides' *Electra*, on the other hand, Electra dominates the action in all but the physical consummation of the deeds. Now the very human motivations of Electra – not only of hatred and vengeance but also of bitter resentment for her own lot and jealousy of her mother – receive the dramatist's greatest emphasis, particularly in the early parts of the play. It may not be too fanciful, then, to suggest that, in the Chorus' retelling and rejection of a tale of divine wrath, the poet is commenting on the more traditional treatment of the vengeance myth of this play, and of his own rejection of such a treatment. If so, Euripides may once again be seen as refashioning current philosophical views to express his own dramatic ideas.

Comparable with this passage from the *Electra* (at least with regard to 'Sophistic' views on the possible origins of theistic belief) is a strange little passage in Euripides' *Hecuba*. Here, the captive Trojan Queen is seeking vengeance against her former ally Polymestor (who has slain her young son, Polydorus, left in his care) for this outrage against the law of hospitality. She appeals for help in this from her former enemy King Agamemnon as the defender (she hopes) of *nomos*, in its earliest sense of 'civilized conduct' and the sanctions governing it:

> We are but slaves, and weak, perhaps. But the gods are strong and *nomos* rules them (*chô keinôn kratôn nomos*). For by *nomos* we believe in the gods, and live our lives defining unjust things and just. (*Hec.* 798-801)

(I shall be referring to this interesting passage again later, in Chapter VI, in the context of several Euripidean passages relating to *nomos* and to Sophistic views on this concept.)

In the first episode of Euripides' *Bacchae*, Teiresias, the aged priest of Apollo, seeks, in several passages, to persuade the young King Pentheus of both the rightness and the necessity of accepting the 'new' god, Dionysus, whose divinity Pentheus clearly rejects:

> Among men, my son, there are two primal matters, the goddess *Demeter* (she is Earth, *Ge*, call her whichever name you wish). She nourishes men with dry substance. (*Bacch.* 274-7)

> He who came afterwards, the son of Semele [i.e. Dionysus] discovered the matching draught of the grape cluster, and introduced it to men. This draught relieved poor men of pain and trouble ... (*Bacch.* 279-81)

> This one [Dionysus], being himself a god (*theos gegôs*) is poured out in libation to the gods (*theoisi spendetai*), so that, through this, they may receive his good. (*Bacch.* 284-5)

This is the clearest expression in a Euripidean play either

of the identification of a god both with a beneficent substance (Demeter and Dionysus, respectively, at 274-7 and at 284-95), or with its discoverer (Dionysus, at 279-81).

A similarly clear expression of both these ideas is found in two passages reporting the teachings of the Sophist Prodicus – not, it is true, of his own views but of what he believed 'the ancients' (*hoi palaioi*) thought:

> The ancients thought [according to Prodicus] that all things useful to our life were gods on account of their usefulness ... and that for this reason bread was called Demeter, wine Dionysus, water Poseidon, fire Hephaestus, and so on for all the most useful things.
>
> (D-K 84 B5, in part)

Thus far Sextus' account (*Adv. Math.* ix.18). Philodemus (c. 9, 7 p. 75 G) tells us further that (still according to Prodicus):

> ... later (*meta de tauta*) those *discovering* means of nourishment or [inventing] shelters and other devices were considered gods, as, for example, Demeter and Dionysus ... (D-K 84 B5, in part; my italics)

(There is, indeed, a fragment [88 B6] in which Critias, a contemporary of Prodicus, himself *identifies* a favourable human condition with a god: 'health ..., the most delightful of the gods to mortals.' However, the context indicates fairly clearly that this is merely a metaphorical rather than a literal identification.)

The comparison between Teiresias' statements about Demeter and Dionysus and the fragment (D-K 84 B5) of Prodicus has already been made by Dodds, though he does not cite the second part of Prodicus' teaching quoted above.[16]

With these statements about the gods in Euripides' *Bacchae* and in Prodicus' account of the views of 'the ancients', we may also compare one or two other Euripidean and Sophistic passages apparently 'identifying' a god with a phenomenon or a human emotion.

In Euripides' *Hippolytus*, the Nurse, shocked that her chaste mistress Phaedra could, however unwillingly, have fallen in love with her step-son, cries out:

> Cypris [i.e. Aphrodite], then you were not a god at all,
> but if there is anything stronger than a god ...
> (*Hipp.* 359-60)

Indeed, in the whole play it might well be said that 'Aphrodite' *is* heterosexual passion, as in the fragment of Antiphon 87 B17 quoted below, rather than that she 'represents' it, or is 'the goddess of it'. Even in the Prologue, when Aphrodite says of Hippolytus, '... he says that I am the basest of the gods; he forswears sex and will have naught to do with marriage' (*anainetai de lektra kou psauei gamôn*, 14), she comes as close to such self-identification by a goddess with what we would regard as an impersonal force, as is possible in a play; the very words which the goddess chooses tend to support this impression.

A comparable ambiguity about Aphrodite occurs in Euripides' *The Trojan Women*, when Hecuba, sneering at Helen's excuse that it was Aphrodite who forced her to elope with Paris, declares:

> Your mind (*nous*) on seeing him [Paris] *became* Cypris (*epoiêthê Kypris*). For all human beings' follies are their 'Aphrodite', and the name *aphrosunê* [folly] rightly shows the root sense of the goddess. (*Tro.* 988-90)

This pun (*Aphroditê/aphrosunê*), involving a play on both sound and sense, was a kind particularly beloved of Euripides and the Sophists. Aeschylus was also fond of such puns, e.g. in the plays on Helen's name at *Ag.* 689-90).

There is also one other Sophistic passage which one might compare with these. Harpocration, the Alexandrian lexicographer, quotes Antiphon as using 'Aphrodite' for the first time as the word for 'sexual pleasure' (D-K 87 B17).

From the foregoing assortment of passages one may readily infer that Euripides is exploiting various Sophistic ideas (most notably, perhaps, those of Prodicus) about the gods and the origins of myths about them; in each case, he adapts and develops these ideas to suit his own dramatic theme without strict regard for historical accuracy.

II

The Nature and Teachability of Virtue

SOME SOPHISTIC VIEWS

Let us begin, then, with certain Sophistic views (and, in one instance, an indication of 'Socrates' view) on 'virtue' (*aretê*) and on virtues of various kinds in various contexts.

Since the Sophists were the first professional teachers of virtue at Athens, the question whether virtue (*aretê*) actually *is* teachable, or whether it comes by some other means, is, of course, of considerable importance. The clearest example of Sophistic claims on this matter occurs near the beginning of Plato's *Protagoras* (at *Prt.* 317Bff.= D-K 80 A5):

> [Protagoras] I have then travelled a different road from other men and I agree that I am a Sophist and that I teach men ... and indeed I have practised this art for many years ... (317 B-C) ... My teaching concerns advice about domestic matters, how one may best arrange his household, and advice about political matters, how one may best conduct and discuss the affairs of the city ... (318D) ... [Socrates] ... for you seem to me to mean the political art and to promise to make men good citizens. – This is indeed the case, Socrates, he replied (319A). [Socrates] ... you then declare quite openly to all the Greeks that you are a Sophist, so naming your-

self, and that you are a teacher of virtue and you declare that you are the first to be worthy to receive pay for this (349A).

Socrates does not, of course, agree with Protagoras' account of this matter. Indeed the whole long argument of the *Protagoras* leads to Socrates' demonstration that no 'virtue' is a specific art (*technê*) which can be taught as such, but that all the virtues, 'temperance' (*sôphrosunê*), 'justice' (*dikaiosunê*), 'piety' (*hosiotês*), and 'courage' (*andreia*), are one, and that that one is 'knowledge' (*sophia*). In the end, then, Socrates does reach the conclusion that 'virtue', viewed in these terms, *is* teachable (*Prt.* 360E).

We should note also (for the point will be relevant to one of the Euripidean passages to be considered) that, in the course of his establishment of the primacy of knowledge as subsuming all the virtues, Socrates spends a good deal of time (*Prt.* 353Aff.) refuting the popular view that such knowledge can be overthrown by pleasure or pain or by emotions such as anger, so that a man, though he knows 'what is best', fails to do it.[1]

Another Socratic dialogue in which the question of the 'teachability' of virtue arises (in a somewhat different context), is the *Meno*. Though no conclusive answer is given there (we are told [99E] at the end of the dialogue 'We must first inquire what virtue is'), nevertheless, the way in which Meno introduces the topic sheds light on the ways in which virtue was discussed in the Sophistic period. 'Can virtue be taught?' Meno asks Socrates, '... or does it come by practice? Or ... do people get it by nature [*phusei*] or in some other way?' (*Meno* 70A). We shall find this choice of views to be relevant to several of the Euripidean passages to be considered, e.g. *Hipp.* 79-80, 373ff., 916-22.

A rather different feature of Sophistic teaching related to the treatment of virtue was the insistence on precise and singular definition of the meanings of words, especially of technical terms. Prodicus was the teacher particularly associated with this interest and there are several passages in Plato's dialogues where it is mentioned, sometimes a shade satirically, as if it were something of an obsession with that particular Sophist. (See, for example, *Prt.* 337A and *Laches* 197B = D-K 84 A13 and 84 A17, respectively). It is true that this concern for precise definition belonged more to rhetorical training than to ethical teaching about virtue. Nevertheless, it had its relevance to the latter as well, since it included precise definitions of ethical terms, and precise meanings of various virtues. Once again, examples will be found at *Laches* 197B-D = D-K 84 A17), where Laches is represented as distinguishing 'fearlessness' (*to aphobon)* from 'courage' (*andreia*), and 'courage' from 'daring' (*thrasutês*) – and to have derived this doctrine indirectly from Prodicus:

> [Nicias] But 'fearlessness' [*to aphobon*] and 'courage' (*to andreion*) are not the same, for I think that only a few have a share in courage and foresight, while many share in fearlessness and lack of foresight ... (197B) ... [Socrates] Don't answer him, Laches, for you don't seem to realize that he [Nicias] has picked up this cleverness from our comrade Damon. For Damon frequently associates with one Prodicus who seems to me of all the Sophists to distinguish most marvellously (*kallista*, in a sarcastic sense?) between terms (*onomata*) of this kind (197D).

This concern with precise definitions will also find its echo in Euripides and it is interesting to note that according to one tradition the dramatist was said to have listened to Prodicus' lectures; see Prodicus (D-K 84 A8).

Concern for the precise meanings of words was not, of course, limited to Prodicus among the Sophists. Evidence of such interest occurs in several fragments of other Sophists and in ancient references to their teachings. Of these, the terms *kairos*, *aidôs* and *sôphrosunê* are of particular relevance to our study.

ho kairos, in the sense of 'the timely', 'the appropriate', had for long been an important concept in Greek thought. Chilon, one of the so-called 'Seven Wise Men', is quoted by Critias (D-K 88 B7) as saying: 'Nothing in excess: all fine things belong only to the right moment' (D-K 10 e1) (*mêden agan: kairôi panta prosesti kala*). One of the sayings attributed to Pittacus, another of 'the Seven', was *gnôthi kairon*: 'Know the right moment.' There are several sayings of Democritus, not a Sophist but a contemporary of the Sophists, which stress *ho kairos*, e.g. at D-K 68 B94, 'Small favours at the right moment become great ones' (*mikrai charites en kairôi megistai*) and at B87, where he speaks of the necessity of seizing 'the opportunity' (*kairou labein*) and B226 where *tou kairou diagnôsis* means 'recognizing the right occasion' or 'the right moment'.

That the Sophists also made much of *ho kairos*, presumably in an ethical context, appears from several fragments and fragmentary references. Thus Diogenes Laertius says of Protagoras, 'He first set down the importance, or power (*dunamis*), of *kairos*.' Dionysius of Halicarnassus, on the other hand, says of our term: 'No orator or writer up till now has defined the art (*technê*) of *kairos*, not even Gorgias of Leontini who tried to write concerning it and wrote nothing worthwhile [about it].' In the fragment from Critias quoted above (D-K 88 B7), it is not quite clear whether the statement involving *kairos* belongs to the quotation of Chilon or to

Critias' comment on it. In either case, Critias' interest in, and emphasis on, the concept is indicated. Finally (and perhaps most significantly, as we shall see, for our purposes), the author of the *Dissoi Logoi* sums up his 'proofs' that the same things are both shameful (*aischra*) and noble [or seemly, *kala*] by saying: 'Everything done at the right moment is seemly, at the wrong moment, shameful (*panta kairôi men kala enti, en akairiai d'aischra*, D-K 90.2.20). It is interesting that this passage of the *Dissoi Logoi* follows immediately after an anonymous quotation of four iambic verses which run as follows (and which one editor, Valkanaer, regards as Euripidean):

> For, if you distinguish things in this way you will discern another law for mortals: nothing is either seemly (*kalon*) or base (*aischron*) in every circumstance, but the right moment (*ho kairos*), taking the same things and transforming them, makes the base seemly and the seemly base. (D-K 90.2.19)

That the two other ethical (and to some degree related) ethical terms which we have mentioned, namely *aidôs* and *sôphrosunê*, ('a sense of shame' or 'of respect' and 'self-control' or 'modesty', to give them their most basic meanings), were also important in philosophic discussions of Euripides' time, also appears from several pre-Socratic fragments and references. Democritus (D-K 68 B179) appears to equate *aidôs* with *aretê* in general and to recommend the traditional education of the young (i.e. grammatical, musical and athletic training) as tending to produce it. In Plato's *Protagoras*, Protagoras is represented as relating, in his mythical account of the origin of civilization, that Zeus sent Hermes with the gifts of *aidôs* and *dikê* ('justice') as the two virtues necessary to enable men to live together in civic harmony. (See Plato, *Protagoras* 320Cff. = D-K 80 C1). It is true, of course, that we have no direct evidence that this was actually Protagoras' own mythical account; be that as it may, it seems unlikely that Plato would associate the term *aidôs* with the Sophist's teaching, in so important a context, if he had not shown interest in the significance of this virtue.

With regard to *sôphrosunê*, there are several fragments of Antiphon which are of interest to us for several reasons; not only do they indicate the Sophists' interest in the significance of this word, and in the different meanings which might be given to it, but also the terms in which the virtue is discussed in two of the fragments are of particular relevance to certain Euripidean passages soon to be discussed. In Antiphon D-K 87 B58, *sôphrôn* is used in the sense of 'prudent', 'possessed of forethought', and a fairly commonplace example is given of this (as we shall see) by no means comprehensive meaning of the word. At the end of the same passage (from Stobaeus III.20.66), however, the meaning is broadened to include 'self-control', particularly of the man who withstands the immediate pleasures of his desire (or 'spirit': *thumos*). Finally, at B59, we are told:

> Whoever neither desires nor touches (*hêpsato*) what is shameful and evil, is not *sôphrôn*. For not having conquered anything, he has not made himself well-behaved (or 'well-ordered': *kosmios*) by overcoming anything.

This last fragment we shall find to be of particular interest for one of the Euripidean passages to be discussed (*Hipp.* 730-1).

VIRTUE IN *HIPPOLYTUS*

Among Euripides' plays, it is the *Hippolytus* which (some readers may be surprised to discover) most frequently reflects the ethical concerns suggested by the philosophical fragments just discussed. True, an outline of the tragic action, of what *happens* in the play, does little to indicate this. Its main theme is, of course, the vengeance of Aphrodite, goddess of love, against the chaste hero Hippolytus, who will have none of her. To execute this vengeance, the goddess causes Phaedra, Hippolytus' stepmother, to fall in love, against her will, with the hero. When King Theseus, Phaedra's husband, learns of this (so Aphrodite plans, though this is not precisely what Theseus learns), he will destroy Hippolytus by one of the three effective curses bestowed on him by the god Poseidon. The catastrophe planned by Aphrodite is fulfilled, though just *how* it happens is determined (with the one exception of Phaedra's god-induced passion) entirely by human reactions to, and human misunderstandings of, the situation. (The vengeance of Aphrodite itself *can,* of course, be interpreted in human or psychological terms, but that is not the question with which we are here concerned.) It is in this human activity, and in the nature and reflections of the human characters involved, that the various ethical themes, adopted (in my view) from Sophistic and Socratic discussions, make their appearance.

Hippolytus' Prologue prayer (which follows Aphrodite's terrifying annonouncement of her plan for vengeance) is addressed to the goddess Artemis:

> O mistress, I bring you this garland, which I have woven for you from the virgin (*akeratos*) meadow, where no

> plough has entered and no shepherd has ever dared to feed his flocks, but only the bee in springtime has approached this untouched (*akeratos*, again) field. And *Aidôs* ('reverence') nourishes it with her river waters. And only those for whom chastity (*to sôphronein*), in no wise taught, is a part of their nature have the right to cull blossoms there; to wicked ones it is not permitted. (*Hipp.* 73-81)

The words *aidôs* and *sôphrosunê*, or their cognates, are both ones which, as we have noted, recur in Sophistic discussions of virtue. Here (and at 667, 994, 1007, 1034-5, 1365) Hippolytus uses *sôphrosunê* and its cognates in praise of his own chaste nature, and *aidôs* to express his reverence for Artemis, goddess of chastity. Both terms, as we shall see, are to recur in significantly different contexts throughout the play. So, too, the word *semnos* is to undergo similar variations ('holy',/'haughty' or even 'pompous') in ethical contexts, one of them (at 1364) in connection with *sôphrôn*. Immediately after Hippolytus' Prologue speech, Hippolytus' Servant timidly uses the expression *to semnon* in the sense of 'disdain' or 'haughtiness', of Hippolytus' dangerous attitude toward Aphrodite (93). Significantly, he uses the same word (*semnê*, 99), a moment later, in the sense of 'august', 'holy', to describe Aphrodite: a significant indication early in the play that this word, in its honorific sense, should be used only of the gods, and not (as Hippolytus is to use it later of himself, 1364) of mortals. By the same token Theseus is later (1064) to use *semnos* sneeringly of Hippolytus as of one claiming more than human virtue. This ambiguous, almost contradictory, use of *semnos* and *sôphrôn* reminds us of the importance attached by Prodicus and other Sophists to precise terminology, especially in discussions of virtue, and we are to note, as the play develops, a still more ambiguous treatment of the word *aidôs*. It is almost as if Euripides were drawing attention, for dramatic reasons of his own, to this particular Sophistic concern.

That Phaedra should here be a virtuous and unwilling victim of the scourge of love for her step-son (unlike the Phaedra of Euripides' earlier version of the myth) is an essential feature of this play. The revelation of her suppressed and secret passion is also, of course, essential to the tragic denouement. This revelation is made by Phaedra to the Nurse (not by Aphrodite to Theseus, as the goddess has seemed to imply at 42 in the Prologue that it will). It takes place, moreover, despite the apparently god-driven plot of this tragedy, in a way directly related to the moral issues and ethical problems with which we are at present concerned.

In her first appearances we see Phaedra hysterical with suppressed love but steadfastly refusing to reveal her guilty secret to the sympathetic Chorus or to the Nurse. Only when the Nurse employs the device of formal supplication does Phaedra (reluctantly? there is perhaps some ambiguity on this point) give in:

> I will grant your request: for I stand in awe of your suppliant hand (*sebas gar cheiros aidoumai to son*).
>
> (*Hipp*. 335)

The revelation has been made against Phaedra's better judgment and is, of course, to have disastrous consequences. Significantly, it is Phaedra's *aidôs* (here in the sense of 'awe' or 'respect' for religious convention), ostensibly a 'good' quality, which proves her undoing.

After the Nurse has left the stage in horrified (but short-lived) moral outrage, Phaedra turns to the Chorus with an account of her situation and of how she has sought to deal with it. First, however, she indulges in a philosophic disquisition on the causes of human wrong-doing. This passage (however improbable it might appear dramatically)[2] is one of great intrinsic interest as well as of considerable relevance to our subject:

> Troezenian women, ... ere now I have wondered vainly in the long watches of the night just in what way the life of mortals gets corrupted. They seem to me to follow the worse course (*prassein kakion*) not through the nature of their judgment (*ou kata gnômês phusin*), for many have good moral judgment, but rather the matter should be tracked down in this way: we learn and come to know what is best (*ta chrêsta*) but we do not labour at it, some through idleness, others through choosing some pleasure in place of what is right (*anti tou kalou*), for there are many pleasures in life, long conversations and leisure, a wicked indulgence ... and then there is *aidôs*.[3] Now there are two kinds of *aidôs*, the one not bad, the other the bane of houses. If *ho kairos* [in this matter] were clear, there would not be two different things [i.e. the two kinds of *aidôs*] having the same letters. (*Hipp*. 373-87)

Readers of Euripides will recognize this passage as one providing several interpretative difficulties and ambiguities which have been discussed in great detail by scholars. Most of these interpretative details are beyond the scope of the present study. For our purposes it will suffice to observe in the passage the surfacing of certain topics and terms prominent, to a greater or lesser degree, in Sophistic and Socratic discussions already summarized.

First of all, of course, Phaedra's discussion of the relation (or lack of it) between judgment or understanding (*gnômê*) and good conduct must remind us of the contrasting Socratic doctrine *equating* virtue and knowledge, and particularly of Socrates' discussion of this issue in his debate with Protagoras on the teachability of virtue at *Protagoras* 352Bff. That the present passage reflects such discussions (not necessarily, of course, any specific debate such as that recreated by Plato in the *Protagoras*!) seems all the more clear from two further points: first, the fact that Phaedra expresses her view in argumentative form (e.g. not A but B seems to me to be the case), and secondly, the fact that at least one of Phaedra's explanations of 'wrong-doing despite understanding' (i.e. through the distractions of pleasure) coincides with the rejection of this very explanation in the view attributed to 'Socrates'. One need not, of course, regard the passage as arguing against the Socratic view, or even as expressing the poet's own contribution to the debate on these matters.[4] All that I would claim in this connection is that Euripides is exploiting for his own dramatic purposes an ethical theme of intense contemporary interest. We shall see as well that this is no meretricious exploitation aimed at seeking the audience's interest; rather, the implications of Phaedra's reflections are to have a bearing on the thematic material of the whole tragedy.

To this conventional explanation (i.e. 'the distractions of pleasure') of why men fail to do the good they know, Phaedra adds an unusual one: '... and *aidôs*'. Now *aidôs* in its good (and most usual) senses – 'awe', 'respect', 'piety' (the sense in which Hippolytus has used it in his Prologue prayer to Artemis), 'a sense of shame' – may generally be regarded as keeping men from violent or shameful actions. (It is in this sense too that Protagoras, in Plato's dialogue, uses it in treating it as one of the civilizing virtues which keep men from mutual destruction.) What, then, can be that other *aidôs*, which Phaedra describes as 'the bane of houses'? One might be tempted to think of it as 'scandal' or 'that which *causes* shame' (the secondary sense of *aidôs*), except that *aidôs* in that sense would hardly fit Phaedra's inclusion of it (along with other distractions) as something which inhibits right action. Since there would appear to be no sense of *aidôs* which would *generally* be regarded as fulfilling both these requirements, one is led to think that Phaedra is now moving from the general ethical reflections with which she began her speech to reflection on the special case of her own situation. In that case we can indeed see a way in which *aidôs* fits both aspects of Phaedra's discussion. In the preceding scene Phaedra has twice (at 219 and 229 respectively) warned the Nurse that her persuasions will be the ruin of her mistress. Now, as we see from 335 ('I stand in awe [*aidoumai*] of your suppliant hand'), she finally succumbs to the Nurse's *formal* supplication that she reveal her secret. Thus, as her use of *aidoumai*, the verbal form of *aidôs*, indicates, Phaedra allows her sense of conventional piety or respect to overcome her judgment as to what is right. And this will also be, as Phaedra foresees, a case in which *aidôs* will indeed prove to be 'the bane of houses'.[5] We now see, as well, how Phaedra's reference to *ho kairos* (another key ethical term) at 386-7 is particularly relevant to the present situation: the distinction between the good and the bad *aidôs* depends, in the case of such conventional observances, on the rightness, or otherwise, of the occasion.[6]

I have lingered on the interpretation of *Hipp.* 385-7, by now rather a commonplace in Euripidean studies, mainly in order to illustrate the Sophistic ambiguities implied in the passage. Thus we have now noted in Phaedra's initial ponderings on her situation several issues which we have also observed as prominent in contemporary philosophic thought. We have noted first of all Phaedra's rejection, or at least qualification, of the relation between virtue and knowledge or understanding, so important to the question of the teachability of virtue. We have noticed also the Queen's concern, such as the Sophists also showed, for the precise meaning and application of ethical terms, and her emphasis on two ethical concepts (*aidôs* and *ho kairos*) in which the Sophists also showed particular interest. As we shall see, the way in which various ethical terms and concepts are used, in different contexts, both here and in Hippolytus' Prologue scene, are to combine to provide a single web of meaning before the tragedy is over.

In the rest of this long speech (373-430) to the Chorus, Phaedra explains her motive, namely her good reputation (*eukleia*) and that of her family, for suppressing her illicit passion and all public knowledge of it. Yet even as she so resolves, her conventional (and badly timed) pious respect (*aidôs*) for the Nurse's suppliant hand breaches that very secret which she would otherwise have taken to the grave. Thus Phaedra, despite her subtle understanding of the struggle for virtue as she understands it, fails in her final attempt to achieve it.

What of Hippolytus, with his much simpler view of virtue as something which comes by nature and not by teaching (79-81)? Hippolytus' much-prized virtue is, in turn, to be shown as self-delusion. When the Nurse, against her mistress's wishes, reveals Phaedra's secret passion to him, Hippolytus delivers his famous tirade against all womankind, ending with the cry, 'Let someone teach them to be chaste (*sôphronein*) or let me trample on them forever!' (667-8). Hippolytus' words here and throughout the whole tirade are, of course, a direct contradiction (as Dodds has shown) of the larger meanings ('moderation', 'self-control') of the hero's much-vaunted virtue of *sôphrosunê.* And it is also this speech, which the

Queen overhears, that leads Phaedra to incriminate Hippolytus as her seducer in a lying suicide note to her husband Theseus. Appropriately, it is left to Phaedra, in her final lines, to spell out for the audience the full significance of Hippolytus' self-damning words:

> But in dying I will become a bane to that other one as well, that he may learn not to be lofty (*hupsêlos*) about my troubles. And in sharing with me this fatal illness, he will learn true understanding (lit. 'how to be truly *sôphrôn*' – *sôphronein mathêsetai*). (*Hipp.* 728-31)

A comparable, though in this case ironic, instance of rejection of Hippolytus' claim to *sôphrosunê* comes from Theseus, when, believing Phaedra's lying letter, he assails his son for his alleged seduction of his step-mother:

> So you're that *sôphrôn* one, quite untouched (*akeratos*) by evil. Go on now with your boasting, your trafficking in meatless diet, your life of fasting! You won't deceive *me*!
> (*Hipp.* 949-53, in part)

Clearly Theseus' accusations here are technically unjust, for Hippolytus *is sôphrôn* in the sense ('chaste') which is here in question. Nevertheless, one feels that Theseus is questioning Hippolytus' claims to *sôphrosunê* in the broader sense as well; for a little later, in the heated dialogue which ensues, he declares, 'Alas! how that pompous piety (*to semnon*) of yours will be my death!' (1064)

Like many, though not all, tragic heroes (Creon in Sophocles' *Antigone* is a notable exception) Hippolytus never learns his lesson. Even as he is dragged dying onstage in the final scene, he still proclaims his virtue:

> ... Zeus, Zeus, do you see this? 'Tis I, the pious (*semnos*), god-fearing one, the one who surpasses all in chastity (*sôphrosunê*), who rushes headlong down to Hades!
> (*Hipp.* 1363-6)

So Hippolytus, no more than Phaedra, succeeds in achieving the virtuous life (or, perhaps, in Phaedra's case, the virtuous death) to which each aspired. And in the denial to the chaste Hippolytus (particularly by Phaedra at 728-31) of the true virtue of *sôphrosunê*, we are reminded of Antiphon's explanation (D-K 87 B59) why he who has never desired nor touched what is shameful and evil is not *sôphrôn*.[7]

Enough has been said, perhaps, to show that Euripides has provided, as a sort of running motif beneath his tragic theme, a constant questioning of the Sophistic claim to the teachability of virtue, and even (though more tentatively) of the Socratic claim that it is a part of wisdom. This sub-motif indeed surfaces for a moment in a curious little passage, a sort of lull before the storm, at the beginning of the scene between Theseus and Hippolytus from which I have just been quoting. Too outraged for the moment even to vent his fury directly on his son, Theseus 'philosophizes' his indignation in typically Euripidean manner:

> O mortal creatures, you who vainly go astray in so many ways, why do you teach countless skills (*technai*), contrive and discover all manner of things, and yet this one thing you do not know and have not hunted down, namely how to teach sound, virtuous judgment (*phronein*) to those who haven't got good sense (*nous*). (*Hipp.* 916-20)

And Hippolytus (unaware of the direction of his father's outburst) replies:

> That's indeed a clever sophist (*deinon sophistên*) you've mentioned, one who can force those who have *no* sense to have good sense! (*Hipp.* 921-2)

Hippolytus, thinking, no doubt, of lesser mortals than himself, speaks ironically (as Barrett has observed),[8] but the *dramatist's* irony, of course, includes Hippolytus and the whole situation (whether one regards it as human or divine in its causation) which the tragedy of Hippolytus embraces.

III

The Relativity of Virtue

SOME SOPHISTIC VIEWS

The concept of the relativity of 'the good', and so of various traditional 'virtues', was, perhaps, one of the most radical of Sophistic ethical teachings, though (as always when dealing with the Sophists) its documentation is all too limited. Protagoras' celebrated maxim, 'Man is the measure of all things …', though its primary application was, as we shall see, to the nature of reality (objective or otherwise), presumably had ethical implications as well, for it celebrates the primacy of individual perceptions.[1] In a different context (*Prt.* 333D = D-K 80 A22), Plato has Protagoras define 'the good' in terms of 'the useful' and then show that what is not useful, or good, for men may be useful, or good, for horses. That in this passage Plato is reflecting actual Protagorean doctrine, and that it was applicable to ethical teaching, seems probable from the fact that the same idea occurs also in the *Dissoi Logoi* (D-K 90) 1 and 2, the anonymous author of which is thought to have been influenced by Protagoras.[2] In this passage, the author proceeds from morally neutral examples where the same thing may be both bad and good (e.g. illness for the sick man and for the doctor, respectively) to activities which may sometimes be described as 'fine' or 'noble' (*kalon*), sometimes as 'disgraceful' (*aischron*), depending on the circumstance, the occasion and even the nationality of the participants. (It is true that the examples of 'the disgraceful' tend to lump together offences against propriety, such as women washing themselves in the *gymnasia*, and moral offences, such as adultery and incest.) It is interesting that in this connection the anonymous author quotes a (likewise anonymous) passage of four iambic trimeters, which one editor (Valkenaer), at least, considers to be Euripidean, and which expresses a similar view:

> For, if you examine things in this way you will find this other 'law' (*nomos*) for mortals which goes like this: there is nothing noble or base (*kalon* ... *aischron*) but the right occasion (*ho kairos*) takes the same things and makes the base noble and the noble base.
>
> (D-K 90.2.19 = *TGF* 844, *adesp.* 26)

Comparable, though by no means identical with these arguments concerning the relative goodness or badness of an action depending on its circumstances (and so, presumably, concerning the relativity of virtue in general), is the more radically iconoclastic position of Antiphon who (as revealed in a substantial papyrus fragment (D-K 87 B44) provides several examples 'to demonstrate that many of the things which are just according to law are at variance with nature'.[3] Antiphon goes on to recommend the things in accord with nature as more advantageous and pleasant than the things according to law. In another passage of the same long fragment, Antiphon provides an example of what he considers to be contradictory principles of justice: 'giving evidence against one's neighbour' and 'not wronging one who has not wronged you'; 'either *one* of these is just,' he argues, 'or both are unjust' (B44, B). Antiphon concludes: 'It is clear that the administration of law and justice and arbitration ... are all contrary to justice.'

Finally, with these other Sophistic examples of the relativity of *to agathon* and *to kalon* and of apparently contradictory ethical situations, we may cite again that fragment from Critias (D-K 88 B7) which we quoted in our examples of *ho kairos*: 'All that is fair (*panta* ... *kala*) depends on the right moment (*kairôi*).'

In the passages quoted or referred to above, some of the illustrations showing how the same things may be both good and evil, noble and disgraceful, may strike us as obvious, even banal. Nevertheless, the central point is that the Sophists generally appear, on the one hand, to have questioned the absolute value of specific traditional virtues, or virtuous activities, and, on the other hand, to have introduced the important philosophical/ethical idea that what in some circumstances was traditionally considered virtuous might in other circumstances prove to be the opposite.

THE '*CHARIS*-THEME' IN *ALCESTIS* AND *HELEN*

Various issues and discussions in Euripides' plays seem to involve this Sophistic view of the relativity of ethical values. The treatments of *aidôs* and *sôphrosunê* in the *Hippolytus* have surely such a bearing: what is *sôphrôn* to Hippolytus, for example, does not seem so to Phaedra (see *Hipp.* 567-8 and 731, respectively). These and similar passages have a bearing on another concern of certain Sophists: the definition, or precise meaning, of various qualities, including 'virtues', and it is in this connection that I have discussed them earlier.[4] However, perhaps the best, or at any rate the most fruitful, examples of Euripides' original treatments of the relativity of virtue are provided by his various dramatizations of the *charis* (or 'favour for favour') theme.

In the two plays which we shall now consider in this connection, the treatments of *charis* illustrate this Sophistic relativism in quite different ways, in the different contexts involved. In the *Alcestis*, the ironic and potentially tragic treatment of *charis* is a serious part of the ethical meaning of the play. In the *Helen*, *charis* is treated with tragi-comic wit in the gulling of Theoclymenus by Helen and Menelaus. Later, in our next chapter, when we consider various aspects of rhetoric presented in *Hecuba*, we shall see another, again quite different, example of the 'relativistic' treatment of *charis*, where this virtue seems to be defined in terms of the self-interest of the speaker.

It has long been recognized that the *Alcestis*, as a 'pro-satyric' play (as seems suggested by its second *Hypothesis* and by its subject-matter), occupies a place somewhere between tragedy and comedy. (The term 'tragi-comedy', however, hardly does justice to the consistently ironic tone, 'the dry mock', as one critic has termed it, maintained throughout.) Thus the *Alcestis* is uniquely well suited to the Sophistic treatment (as described above) of certain traditional Greek ethical values. The values here concerned are *charis* ('favour') and *xenia* ('hospitality'), in both of which the reciprocal nature of the activity between the participating parties is always, or almost always, implied or understood. The following brief summary will indicate how the varied deployment of *charis* and *xenia* is essential to the theme of the play. Both motifs are introduced in the Prologue, where we learn that Apollo, grateful for King Admetus' hospitable treatment during his enforced thralldom, has persuaded the Fates to accept a substitute for Admetus' fated death. Here, too, we learn that only Alcestis is willing to make this sacrifice. For this favour

Alcestis, not unreasonably, demands, in the first episode, 'not an equal favour (*charis*), for nothing is more valuable than life, but still a just one ...' (300-2), namely that Admetus should never marry a new wife to be step-mother over their children. Admetus, oppressed with guilty grief, promises not only this but a life of mourning, with no more 'conivial gatherings, garlands and music' such as used to fill his halls (343-4).

Enter Heracles (shortly after Alcestis' inevitable death), the traditional hearty guest whose very presence implies that conviviality which Admetus, as part of the *charis* due to Alcestis, has promised to forego. Despite the Chorus' disapproval, the King, suppressing news of Alcestis' death, welcomes Heracles as his guest, thus sacrificing the *charis* he owes to Alcestis to the hospitality he owes to Heracles. To the shocked Chorus he explains:

> My misfortune would not have been less [had he turned his guest away] and I would have added another ill: to have my house called inhospitable as well. Besides [he adds significantly] I find this guest to be the best of hosts whenever I go to thirsty Argos. (*Alc.* 555-60)

At the dead centre of this skilfully constructed plot the *charis*-theme apears again, in a scene which contrasts sharply with its initial and final appearances. After Admetus returns, leading Alcestis' funeral procession, his father, Pheres, enters, bearing a tribute for Alcestis in gratitude for ensuring that he would not be deprived of his son in his old age (618-22). Admetus rejects the offering in bitter resentment of the fact that both his parents have refused to die for him despite all the respect and filial piety which he has shown them:

> ... and this is the sort of gratitude which for all this you

> and the one who bore me have repaid me with! (*charin/ toiande ... ellaxatên*, 660-1: this is the only actual occurrence of the word *charis* in the scene).

This scene of rejection provides a sardonic transition between Admetus' ambiguous fulfilment of *charis* to Alcestis and the triumphant fulfilment of the *charis*-theme to which the play's closing scenes will be devoted.

When Heracles discovers the bereaved nature of Admetus' hospitality, he rewards Admetus by struggling victoriously with Death and restoring Alcestis to Admetus' halls. But there is still a further twist: Heracles pretends that the veiled and silent figure of Alcestis is a captive woman, whom he now persuades Admetus to keep for him. Admetus, hospitable to the end, reluctantly agrees to take the woman into his house (1097ff.: their proposed future relationship remains ambiguous) and so his first promise to Alcestis is, at best, compromised. Nevertheless, Admetus' hospitality is rewarded (*charis* for *charis*) a thousandfold when he recognizes that his beloved wife has been restored to him.

Is this primarily a theme of 'hospitality rewarded' (as many critics think), or of *charis* betrayed? Or of *charis* due to one fulfilled at the cost of *charis* to another? Or is the theme all of these at once in Euripides' best ironic manner? However one answers these questions, one can surely agree that the play is a brilliant *tour de force* on a Sophistic theme: the ironic demonstration that even the most accepted of traditional virtues, such as *charis* and *xenia*, are relative to the occasion.

The treatment of *charis* in *Helen* provides a sharp contrast to its ironic treatment in *Alcestis* – and also to its rhetorical treatment in *Hecuba*, to which we shall have occasion to return later. In this fantastic version (borrowed from Stesichorus) of the Helen myth,[5] not Helen but her wraith is carried away to Troy by Paris. Meanwhile, Helen herself is held captive by the wicked King Theoclymenus in Egypt whence she is eventually rescued by Menelaus, after he is shipwrecked (with the wraith of Helen!) on the Egyptian shore.

In the first half of *Helen*, a somewhat difficult 'recognition' is eventually achieved between Menelaus and his long-lost wife, after the wraith of Helen disappears into the heavens. The second half of the play deals with the escape of Helen and Menelaus from Egypt. The *charis*-theme makes its first appearance when Helen persuades the priestess Theonoe against purchasing 'base *charis*' (*charitas ponêras ... onoumenê*, 902, i.e. gratitude basely earned) from her royal brother by providing the wicked favour of revealing the presence of Menelaus.

'Base *charis*' is then treated in farcical terms in the 'deception scene' between Helen and King Theoclymenus. Helen initiates a daring plan for escape with Menelaus (disguised as an anonymous, shipwrecked Greek sailor), by telling a false tale of Menelaus' drowning and adding an equally false promise of marriage to the Egyptian King. 'In return for what?' asks Theoclymenus (unable to believe this good fortune), 'for there should be favour in return for favour (*charis gar anti charitos elthetô*)' (1234). Helen and Menelaus now proceed to take full advantage (unjustly, for Helen will not fulfil the favour *she* has promised) of Theoclymenus' gratitude by tricking the gullible King into aiding their escape. At several points the motif of reciprocal favour is repeated in almost absurd terms (at 1254, 1411, 1420) as the pair reap their full rewards. Indeed, so enamoured is the poet of his play on *charis* that he works it into other contexts as well: that of Theoclymenus' rewarding the disguised Menelaus for 'doing a favour' (*drasanta ... pros charin*, 1281) to Helen, by performing her husband's (supposed) obsequies, and that of the King's fear of the 'charms' (*charis* in an erotic sense) of even the 'deceased' Menelaus (1397). However, Helen finally brings the *charis*-motif, as it functions in the escape plan, to a close with her final false promise to Theoclymenus:

> This day will show my gratitude (*charis*) to you!
> (*Hel.* 1420)

IV

The Power and Abuses of Rhetoric

SOME SOPHISTIC VIEWS

We turn now to a somewhat different aspect of Euripides' employment of Sophistic teachings. The influence of Sophistic rhetoric on Euripides is almost a cliché of literary studies of his plays. This influence is clearly discernible in the structure and the rhetorical devices of the speeches (*rhêseis*), but it extends also to the style of Euripidean drama as a whole. This is particularly true of the markedly 'agonistic' ones, i.e. those in which leading characters indulge in the set speeches of formal debate, involving, for example, political ideologies (as at *Supplices* 409-62), dynastic rivalry (as at *Heraclidae* 134ff.) or personal animosity (as at *Medea* 446ff.).

The technical and stylistic aspects of this area of Sophistic influence on Euripides are beyond the scope of this book. Nevertheless, we need to remember that the influence of Sophistic ideas on Euripides' dramaturgy was part of a larger whole, involving style, language and rhetorical technique. Moreover, since rhetoric formed so large a part of the Sophists' training for 'the good life' (itself associated with political success), it would be surprising if there were not some overlap between their views on rhetoric and their views on 'values' (political and ethical).

One of the major rhetorical claims of the Sophists was that

there were opposite arguments concerning everything (see DK 80 B6a) and even (as Aristotle quotes Protagoras) that they were able 'to make the weaker argument the stronger' (DK 80 B6b). For vivid demonstrations of this Sophistic claim, see Gorgias 82B11, *The Encomium of Helen* (to be discussed below) and, of course, Aristophanes' parody of this claim in the *agôn* of the *Clouds*, the celebrated debate between *Dikaios Logos* and *Adikos Logos*. It is significant that a similar claim seems to have been made by a character in Euripides' *Antiope*:

> If one should be clever at speaking, one should be able to establish a case (*agôna*) consisting of two arguments for every proposition. (*TGF* 189)

Aristotle comments on Protagoras' claim that 'men were justly offended [by this claim], for it is a falsehood and not a true, but only an apparent, probability and in no art (*technê*) except rhetoric and eristic' (D-K 80 A21). So, too, the Platonic Socrates criticizes rhetoric in the *Gorgias* on the grounds that it is concerned with persuasion, not instruction, concerning the just and the unjust (D-K 82 A28=Plato, *Gorgias* 455A). In another passage, Plato quotes Gorgias himself as admitting that under the influence of rhetoric 'all things are willingly ... made slaves' (Plato, *Philebus* 58A: D-K 82 A26).

THE TROJAN WOMEN

The *agônes* of Euripides – formal, often fairly stylized, passages of set debates between two opposed positions or characters – have frequently been celebrated as one of the most characteristic aspects of the dramatist's work. It is also in this part of his plays that, for obvious reasons, reflections of the

Sophists tend to be most marked.[1] Among such passages, the *agôn* of the *Trojan Women* (a set debate between Helen and Hecuba, which shares at least the same subject matter with Gorgias' *Encomium of Helen*) is no exception. However, before commenting on the possible relation between these treatments of an identical issue (the innocence or guilt of Helen), let us glance at an earlier passage in the play which has also been thought to illustrate the Sophistic claim to be able to make the worse argument appear the better.

The situation at the beginning of *The Trojan Women* is that Troy has been sacked, and her heroes slaughtered; the Trojan women (the Chorus in this play) and their Queen, Hecuba, are now being assigned as spoils of war to the victorious Achaean leaders. Cassandra, the crazed, Apollo-inspired daughter of King Priam and Hecuba, has been chosen by Agamemnon. When Cassandra appears, she performs a wild and joyful song and dance celebrating the god Hymen who will preside over her 'wedding'. Then, suddenly and unexpectedly, Cassandra launches into a subtle explanation of how her coming union, and, indeed, the whole Trojan War, is a cause of Achaean grief and Trojan rejoicing.[2] Cassandra prophesies (353ff.) first of all, that her marriage to Agamemnon will actually bring about his death and the ruin of his house. Next (and more significantly for the immediate situation), Cassandra expounds the real truth (as she sees it) about the results of the Trojan War: that it has turned out better for the defeated Trojans than for the victorious Achaeans. The latter died and were buried far from home, while the Trojans died gloriously in defence of their native land. So, too, with the heroes: Hector died 'the best of men' (*anêr aristos*, 395), Paris wed Zeus' daughter, whereas Agamemnon sacrificed *his* beloved daughter for the detested Helen, his brother's wife. (In this paraphrase of Cassandra's long prophetic speech, 353-405, I have slightly changed the sequence of events described.)

As N.J. Croally has well observed of this passage:

> Cassandra at 368ff. adopts a position with no traditional basis to question a traditional fact, i.e. that the Greeks won the Trojan War. One has only to look at Gorgias' *Helen* to see that paradoxical arguments of this nature were one of the characteristics of Sophistic thought.[3]

In the *agôn* of *The Trojan Women*, Helen, now Menelaus' captive, debates with Hecuba for her life. The debate concerning the possible relations between this passage and Gorgias' *Encomium of Helen* has been complicated by uncertainty about the date of Gorgias' work. Some think that it comes between *The Trojan Women* and *Helen*, the majority, with whom I tend to agree, think that it precedes *The Trojan Women*, while a few think it impossible to decide.

Gorgias provides, in his defence of Helen, four possible explanations for her abandoning Menelaus:

> She acted as she did either by the will of Fate, by the designs of the gods and by the dictates of Necessity; or else because she was seized by force; or else because she was deceived by words (or because she was overcome by love).

If we look at the Euripidean Helen's defence (at *Tro.* 914ff.), we will find that the argument about the power of Aphrodite is the only one which also appears in Gorgias' *Encomium*. Helen advanced other arguments: that Paris' preference for *her* over the bribes offered by Hera and Athena saved Greece from conquest by Asia; that Menelaus should not have absented himself when Paris was visiting Sparta; that after Paris' death at Troy, she was forced to marry Deiphobus, and tried unsuccessfully to escape from Troy. But, as far as we know, the Sophists contributed nothing to all this beyond, perhaps, their well-known skill at making good defences of unpromising material, and of course, their general rhetorical influence on Euripidean *agônes* which we have already mentioned. In the latter connection, one passage in Helen's self-defence, *Tro.* 925-34 (Helen's suggestions of what would have happened to Greece if one of the other two goddesses had won Paris' favour with *their* bribes) are little better than 'arguments from probability' which are thought to be a characteristic feature of Sophistic rhetoric.[4]

Hecuba's rebuttal, at *Tro.* 969-1032, also shares (with one possible exception to be noted below) little specific detail with Gorgias' *Encomium.* She rejects Helen's argument that she (Helen) had saved Greece, claiming that Hera would never have bargained away Argos nor Athena allowed her city to fall under the domination of Troy. Furthermore, Aphrodite would not have needed to accompany Paris to Sparta: as a goddess, she could simply have conveyed Helen to Troy. No: Helen's sighting of Paris became *her* 'Aphrodite'. As for Helen's desire to escape from Troy, her behaviour there completely belies such a claim.

Recent critics have held somewhat diverse views about the possible influence of Gorgias' work on this *agôn.* Michael Lloyd claims that such influence is not demonstrable: as we have noted, none of the four causes of Helen's action urged by Gorgias, except for the part played by Aphrodite (and *that* was asserted long before Gorgias), appears in the Euripidean Helen's self-defence.[5]

Ruth Scodel argues intelligently for a general relationship short of 'imitation' between the two passages. Thus, she notes that the ambiguity appearing in the *agôn* of the *Trojan Women* about human or divine reponsibility in erotic matters, is suggestive of Sophistic *dissoi logoi* and is very much a 'fifth-century debate'.[6] Particularly acute are her observations on the Gorgianic echo in *Tro.* 987-90, to which I shall have occasion to refer later.[7] I do not entirely agree, however, with Scodel's conclusion about this scene:

> The criticism of sophistic methods in this scene is not accomplished through a demonstration of its inadequacies, but by a triumphant enactment of one of its arguments.[8]

Surely in this scene Euripides is concerned with dramatic or even theatrical effect, rather than with value judgments about Sophistic method.

As the following quotations will indicate, N.J. Croally, one of the most recent commentators on this scene,[9] finds a relation (though not, perhaps, of a critical kind) between the *agôn* of *The Trojan Women* and Gorgias' *Encomium*:

> Like the speaker in Gorgias' *Helen*, Helen [in Euripides' *agôn*] makes use of traditional religious and cultural notions to demonstrate that she is not responsible [*sc.* for anything that has happened]. For the Chorus, Helen has a sort of Protagorean quality because she can make the guilty position appear innocent ... Both Helen's and Hecuba's arguments employ contemporary fifth-century argumentation.

From our brief summary of the Gorgianic and Euripidean passages, and from the views of at least some Euripidean scholars,[10] there would seem to be a distinct relation between them, which falls short, however, of direct imitation on the poet's part.

There are, however, a few further features of the Euripidean passage which may, perhaps, provide some indication of Euripides' awareness of Gorgias' *Encomium* as he composed this *agôn*, and of his possible intentions with regard to it.

Consider, for example, certain emphases in Helen's introduction to her self-defence:

> Perhaps, *whether I speak well or badly*, you will not cease thinking ill of me. Still, after I have set forth *in my own words* (*dia logôn iont' emou*) what I think that you will charge me with, I shall reply to your accusations with *mine* against *you* (*tois soisi t'ama kai ta s'aitiamata*).
>
> (*Tro.* 914-18)

Here the emphasis on words, and the antithetical expressions used, recall the similar emphasis, similarly expressed, in Gorgias' account of the power of persuasion in his defence of Helen (*Enc.* 13). More significantly, perhaps, Helen's initial emphasis on *aitiamata*, in the context of shifting accusations, or responsibilities, from herself to others, recalls the emphasis on *aitia* in Gorgias' various explanations of the causes of, and shiftings of responsibilities for, Helen's deeds. (See *Enc.* 5, 6, 8, 15 etc.) This part of the Euripidean Helen's argument has, however, certain advantages in immediacy over the Sophist's purely rhetorical pleas, in that Helen can shift responsibility to other characters actually on stage – to Hecuba, for producing Paris and then allowing 'the fire-brand' (as Cassandra had called him) to survive (*Tro.* 919-22), and to Menelaus, for leaving Paris 'an open field', as it were, when he was visiting Sparta (*Tro.* 943-4).

Finally, there is the idea of providing a rebuttal (after Helen's speech) to *any* formal defence of Helen. And who could give this more appropriately than Hecuba, who (for all Cassandra's 'consolations') had lost family and city because of her? This rebuttal, which I have summarized above, provides a very Euripidean reply (first in literal, then in rationalizing terms) to the only part of Helen's defence which appears both in Gorgias' *Encomium* and in Helen's own speech in the present play. It is interesting, too, that in this part of Hecuba's refutation of Helen's arguments, she uses a typically 'Gorgian' description of *seeing as a part of the physical aspect of love*, which Gorgias has used (*Enc.* 15), separately from his 'Aphrodite argument', as one of several ways of exonerating Helen from responsibility for her actions: '... for what we see has a nature which we do not choose ... and through sight (*dia tês opseôs*) the soul is affected even in its ways (*tropois*).' Thus, when we hear Hecuba in the Euripidean passage sarcastically rejecting Helen's 'Aphrodite excuse' with the sneer, 'Your mind on seeing my son's beauty *became* Cypris' (*Tro.* 988), it is tempting to think that Euripides is picking up this Gorgian argument and mischievously using it against Helen instead of for her.[11]

Hecuba's peroration introduces another point relevant to our discussion of Euripides' treatment of this Sophistic theme:

> And you have come forth, before all these assembled here, with your body richly arrayed, and looking up, you shameless one, on the same sky as your husband – you who ought to have come out grovelling and trembling, with tattered clothes and shaven head ...
>
> (*Tro.* 1023-8)

This reference to the *physical appearance* of Helen, as she actually stands before us on the stage, reminds us again of Gorgias' stress on the effect of sight upon the soul (*Enc.* 15), an effect which was available to the dramatic but not to the rhetorical treatment of the debate.

Croally has observed of the *agôn* of *The Trojan Women* that '... there is something of a Euripidean joke in that the ultra-modern Gorgianic discourse [of Helen] is answered by a set of arguments [by Hecuba] perhaps even more contemporary and avant-garde'.[12] This acute comment may not be far from the truth of the matter. However that may be, the scene does, I think, provide us with another example of the poet's conscious and original treatment of a topic celebrated by his Sophistic contemporaries.

HECUBA

Euripides' *Hecuba* in some ways represents, better than any other of his extant plays, the dramatist's reflections on both the power and the abuses of rhetoric, particularly as they appear in the world of *Realpolitik.* Several recent studies have commented on both these features and some of these have also noted the peculiarly anachronistic late fifth-century political tone suggested by certain expressions used.[13]

Hecuba develops, in very different ways, two powerful and related themes, viz. rhetoric (its uses and abuses, and its effects in very different circumstances) and *charis*, that celebrated Greek virtue, 'favour for favour' which, as we have seen, was particularly subject to the ambiguities of Sophistic argument.[14] Both themes are developed in the great rhetorical passages of the play though both are, as we shall see, briefly anticipated in the choral anapaests which introduce the dramatic action.

The play takes place, as does *The Trojan Women*, in the bitter aftermath of the Trojan War and centres on the sufferings of Queen Hecuba, widowed, defenceless and captive of the victorious Greeks. In the first panel of the play, the Greeks sacrifice Polyxena, Hecuba's daughter, to the shade of the slain hero Achilles; in the second, the body of Hecuba's young son (murdered for his gold by Polymestor, his Thracian protector), is cast up on the Trojan shore. These two horrendous events (both anticipated in a Prologue speech by the ghost of the slain Apollodorus), and the Queen's reactions to them, inform the plot around which the rhetorical structure of the play is formed.

In a second Prologue speech, the widowed Queen Hecuba recounts, in the symbolic language of dreams ('... a wolf devouring a dappled fawn, dragged from her own knees', 90ff.) a strange nightmare about these dreadful deeds. Then, in a series of opening anapaests the Chorus of captured Trojan women recount the beginning of the actual event which Hecuba's 'wolf vision' has portended, though their account still belongs to the supernatural world of myth: how the ghost of Achilles appeared in his golden armour (108ff.) and stayed the Achaean fleet from sailing home, with the reproach that they were leaving his tomb unhonoured.

Suddenly, in the Chorus' description, the language changes from the supernatural world of myth to that of fifth-century debate:

> Straightway a wave of contention broke out and diverse opinion (*doxa*) separated the warrior host. To some it seemed best to make sacrifice at Achilles' tomb, to others (*tois men ... tois de*) it did not ... (*Hec.* 116-19)

With the intervention of Odysseus (as the Chorus still recounts events), the themes of 'rhetoric' and '*charis*' make their first appearance. Soon that 'sweet-talking, crowd-pleasing' (*hêdulogos, dêmocharistês*) wrangler' (132) persuades the armed assembly to sacrifice Hecuba's daughter Polyxena at the tomb of Achilles –

> lest anyone should say that the Danaans departed home, ungrateful (*acharistoi*) to those fellow Danaans who died on behalf of Greeks. (*Hec.* 138-40)

With Odysseus' intervention and, indeed, in this whole debate, we seem to be plunged into the world of fifth-century Assembly debates at Athens. Scholars have noted various terms and expressions reminiscent of political and sophistic wrangles, e.g. *dissôn muthôn rhêtores* ('speakers of two-fold arguments'), 123-4; *koina gnôma* ('unanimous opinion'), 188-9, *Argeiôn doxai psêphôi* ('by voted resolution of the Argives') 195-6, in Hecuba's later report of the vote to Polyxena.[15] Thus, while the themes of rhetoric and of *charis*, particularly in a political context, are most frequent in the major speeches of the play, both are neatly anticipated even in these introductory passages.

Hecuba has three great speeches in the play. In the first (251-95) she pleads unsuccessfully with Odysseus to intercede for her daughter's life. In the second (786-845), she pleads (with eventual success) with Agamemnon for help in vengeance on Polymestor. In the third (1188-237), she defends herself before Agamemnon against Polymestor's indictment for her vengeful murder of *his* children. The success or failure of all three of Hecuba's pleas depends on her skill (or lack of it) in the art of persuasion and this in turn involves, in each case, the different effect, in different circumstances and applications, of arguments based on the reciprocal aspect of *charis*.

In her first speech (251-95) Hecuba seeks a favour (*charis*, 276), from Odysseus in return for a favour which she did for him during the Trojan War.

> Are you not shameless with those plans of yours, you who have experienced from us what you admit you have experienced, but who now do us no good but instead do us as much evil as you can! A thankless lot you are, all you who seek honours won by crowd appeal ...
>
> (*Hec.* 251-5)

In the preceding dialogue between them, Hecuba has already claimed, and Odysseus has admitted (239-50), that she had saved his life when she found him spying within the walls of Troy. Now, as often in Euripides' rhetorical treatment of Sophistic themes, the particular is gradually generalized, Hecuba's simple relative pronoun '[you] who (*hos k.t.l.*)' at 252 becoming 'the thankless lot of you who ... (*achariston humôn sperm' hosoi* ...)' at 254. A little later in the same speech, Hecuba makes her 'favour for favour' argument still more specific:

> I ask back and beg of you that favour of former times (*charin t'apaitô tên toth' hiketeuô te se* ... 276) ... not to slay my child.

One further aspect of political rhetoric is highlighted toward the end of Hecuba's appeal that Odysseus use his powers of persuasion in her interest with the armed assembly:

> Your reputation (*axiôma*) even if you speak badly, will

> persuade. For the same argument (*logos*) coming from those of no repute (*adoxountôn*) and those of high repute have not the same effect. (*Hec.* 293-5)

Odysseus answers Hecuba's appeal to her *charis* argument with a speech (299-331) which one critic has aptly characterized as illustrating 'what a virtuoso can do with a really bad case'.[16] The Sophistical quality of Odysseus' answer is anticipated in his opening words, 'Hekabe, let me teach you' (*Hekabê, didaskou*, 299). Hecuba's request of a favour for *her* favour of saving his life, Odysseus is quite willing to fulfil by saving *her* life – which is not, of course, what she is asking. The lesson Hecuba is to learn is that if barbarians (such as the Trojans) requited *their* fallen heroes as the Greeks now propose to honour Achilles, then they would prosper as the Greeks do – and as barbarians do not. This is surely a reply worthy of that arch-Sophist, Aristophanes' *Adikos Logos.* Once again, as in *Alcestis*, circumstances seem to determine, at least for the speaker, the value of *charis.* For Odysseus, political *charis* far outweighs any personal claim.

Polyxena, however, refuses her mother's plea that she too should make supplication to the enemy, Odysseus, as she herself, the noble Queen of Troy, has stooped, for her daughter's sake, to do. A little later, the Herald Talthybius announced the completion of the sacrifice. When Hecuba hears of the bravery with which Polyxena faced death in preference to a life of slavery, she indulges in a typically Euripidean reflection on the causes of human nobility.

> Is it not strange? When poor land gets timely nurture from the heavens, it brings forth good produce, while even the best soil, when it lacks what it needs, yields only a poor harvest. Yet, in the case of humankind, the base

> is always nothing else but base, the noble, noble, and is never corrupted by disaster, but always stays most excellent (*Hec.* 592-8)

Hecuba's words are, however, to be be revealed as tragically ironic by her own reaction to the next disaster. Almost immediately, after a brief choral interlude, the corpse of Polydorus is carried in from the sea-shore, and so Hecuba learns of his murder at the hands of Polymestor, to whose care he had been entrusted.

The second sequence of action, 'the vengeance sequence', now begins, as Hecuba turns to Agamemnon for help in avenging Polydoros' death. In her second great speech (786-845) in the play, the Queen starts (786-811) by appealing to King Agamemnon to defend the sacred law (*nomos*, 800) of hospitality,[17] but in this appeal she fails. As the King turns away, she utters the memorable lines which could later have been used as an enticement for Sophistic schools of rhetoric:

> Why do we mortals work so hard at other skills ... But persuasion, men's only master, the art worth any price to learn, we do not labour to acquire?
> (*Hec.* 814-18, in part)

In desperation, Hecuba now applies a base use of the *charis* argument in the second part of her plea to Agamemnon. She asks his help, 'favour for favour' (*charin*, 830), in return for the sexual favours which her captive daughter Cassandra is bestowing on the King – and thus wins Agamemnon's complicity in her vengeance plan.

Hecuba now wreaks her devastating revenge. She lures Polymestor and his children into her tent with promise of hidden treasure and there the captive Trojan women tear out his eyes and slaughter the children. Polymestor now cries, in turn, to Agamemnon for vengeance on Hecuba, and uses *his* version of the *charis* argument in his appeal:

> ... such agonies have I suffered in seeking to favour you (*speudôn charin*), by slaying an enemy of yours ...
>
> (*Hec.* 175-6)

Hecuba's reply (in her last great speech in the play) is interesting for its use of Sophistic arguments on two major topics of this play, rhetoric and *charis*:

> Agamemnon, it was never right that men should excel more in words than in deed, but rather if one performed noble deeds, it was right that one should also excel in speech, and that if one did base deeds then one's words should also be wretched. One should never be able to dress up unjust deeds in fine words.
>
> (*Hec.* 1187-91)

> And now, against this man I'll reply with words of mine, against *you* who says that to save the Greeks from trouble, and for Agamemnon's sake, you slew my son. O basest of men! How could the barbarian race ever be on terms of friendship with the Greeks? It could not be. In pursuit of what favour (*charin*) then, were you so zealous? Seeking some marriage kin? Or as a relative, perhaps? Or for *what* reason? (*Hec.* 1196-203)

In both these arguments, however rhetorically effective, the Queen would appear to be on somewhat shaky ground. In her own successful plea to Agamemnon, she has been clever rather than good and her sneer that a *barbaros* can hardly claim *charis* from a Greek applies to her claim as well as to Polymestor's.

Hecuba succeeds in her defence against (or is it her indictment of?) Polymestor. Agamemnon, as a somewhat previously 'committed' judge, brusquely dismisses Polymestor's pleas (1240-51). In this last and most successful of her exercises of the art of persuasion, Hecuba shows a renewed and confident power very different from that of the pleading suppliant of the opening scenes. However, her clever use of rhetoric and the sometimes Sophistic arguments she now employs do little to restore the moral stature and dignity which she had shown earlier in her just pleas to Odysseus and, initially, to Agamemnon but which she had lost in her second and successful appeal to him. And, indeed, the very acts of vengeance which she would now justify involve a slaughter of innocents more terrible than the sacrifice of Polyxena.

It is difficult to know just how an Athenian audience of Euripides' day would have viewed Hecuba's deeds in Hecuba's circumstances. Be that as it may, the Hecuba of this final scene compares unfavourably in moral stature with the suffering Queen, widow of Priam and mother of the slain hero, Hector, of the opening scenes. This decline, for which degradation may be too strong a word, is illustrated, perhaps symbolically and certainly theatrically, by Polymestor's extraordinary prophecy at *Hec.* 1265ff. (quoted, he declares, from 'Dionysus, prophet to the Thracians', 1267) of Hecuba's canine metamorphosis. As Collard observes,[18] this transformation into a bitch is 'the archetypal metaphor of shamelessness ... suiting at least Polymestor's view of her [Hecuba]'. But Polymestor did not invent the prophecy and even if this mythical transformation did not originally have a pejorative connotation, Euripides in introducing it at this point would presumably have been aware of this possible impression.

This degeneration (at least in my view) of Hecuba is surely one of Euripides' most bitter dramatizations of the effect of a series of dread catastrophes on a noble character. (It also provides a sort of ironic contradiction of the view expressed by Hecuba herself, when reflecting on Polyxena's death, of the incorruptibility of a noble nature.) The rhetorical motif, on which I have tended to concentrate, pales beside this intensely tragic theme. Nevertheless, I believe that Hecuba's decline is at least reflected, ironically and intentionally by the poet, in the increasing success of her rhetorical efforts at the expense of 'righteousness'. In this sense, then, the characterization of Hecuba might be seen as an indictment of rhetoric perceived as 'the art of persuasion at any cost' – as Gorgias, for example, seems to have perceived it judging from his *Encomium of Helen* and from Plato's representation of his views in *Gorgias* 453A and 455A (= D-K 82 A28).[19]

There has been a wide variety of interpretations of *Hecuba.* Perhaps the majority of these agree that the character of the Queen is presented as undergoing a moral decline as she suffers from her disasters, though not all have presented this decline as I have done. Both Reckford and Nussbaum, for example, tend to give her decline a deeper religious or philosophical dimension, relating it to her loss of confidence in the gods as defenders of *nomos*, as she expresses this at *Hec.* 798ff.[20]

Some more recent commentators, on the other hand, do not accept the 'demoralization view' of the characterization of Hecuba. Mossman, though she gives generous accounts of what she regards as the more popular view (i.e. the 'demoralization view'), argues strenuously against it.[21] Collard also takes a more positive view of Hecuba's characterization than

I have suggested, regarding the Queen's mood as shifting from despair to pride in her vengeance on Polymestor.[22]

The question of Euripides' own attitudes to the various Sophistic teachings behind his Sophistic themes has not, for the most part, been of much concern for the present study. However, in the dramatist's treatment of 'the power and the abuses of rhetoric' (at least as we have seen it in *The Trojan Women* and *Hecuba*), the attitudes expressed seem more closely related to actual Sophistic views and practices than in the other plays considered. This is, perhaps, particularly true of the attitude expressed toward foreigners. In general, it may be presumed that the Sophists, many of whom were foreign intellectuals, were critical of the Athenian conviction of the superiority of Greeks to *barbaroi.* Perhaps the clearest expression of this Sophistic view is to be found in Antiphon D-K 87 B44, where (though Antiphon himself was probably an Athenian) he states that barbarians and Greeks are the same by nature, that all are subject to the same laws of nature and that all breathe and eat in the same way.[23] Euripides' similar rejection of Athenian snobbery in this matter seems clear from several features of *The Trojan Women* and *Hecuba.* In both plays the leading and certainly the most sympathetic characters are the Trojans rather than the Greeks. In *The Trojan Women*, in addition to the contrast between cruel Greeks and suffering Trojans, Helen cuts a sorry figure, morally, in contrast to her debating opponent, Hecuba. In *Hecuba*, Odysseus' claim to Greek superiority over *barbaroi* with respect to honouring fallen comrades, is marred by being part of his heartless argument for refusing Hecuba's plea to save Polyxena from being sacrificed to the shade of Achilles. So, too, in a later passage, Hecuba's appeal to the Greek leader, Agamemnon, to defend *nomos* is singularly unsuccessful, while her appeal to the King's less noble interests prevails.

Finally, in these passages involving 'racial attitudes', we have seen Hecuba (at *Hec.* 1199ff.), before Agamemnon as 'judge', exploiting Greek snobbery by her sneer at the barbarian Polymestor for presuming to claim friendship, involving *charis*, with the Greeks. Thus, on the basis of these two plays alone, Croally surely represents the view of most readers of Euripides when he speaks of the dramatist and the Sophists sharing a challenge to this Athenian view of Greek-barbarian polarity.[24] A somewhat different view has, however, been expressed by Hall, to whom Croally also refers in this connection. She proposes the view that 'Tragic rhetoric often treats the invented barbarian as a single category embodying the opposite of Hellenic values ...'; she has already mentioned 'the avaricious and mendacious Polymestor [in *Hecuba*], and the cowardly Phrygian in *Orestes*' as Euripidean examples of this.[25] However Hall also recognizes later that several characters in Euripidean drama, in particular characters in his 'Trojan plays', *are* 'invested with Hellenic virtues'. One is grateful to Hall for her reminder concerning the *wicked* Euripidean barbarians and for the discussion throughout her fourth chapter of the 'the polarization of Hellenism and barbarism' which she finds in Greek Tragedy. However, I cannot agree that the 'more Hellenic' barbarians in Euripides are exceptions made mainly for 'simple dramatic expediency'.

With regard to Euripides' attitudes to actual Sophistic uses and abuses of rhetoric, the treatments of rhetoric in *The Trojan Women* and in *Hecuba*, respectively, suggest rather different approaches and intentions. In the *agôn* of the former play, the kinds of similarities and differences which we have noted between it and Gorgias' *Encomium*, and the superior vividness and, perhaps, effectiveness, of the Euripidean passage, would seem to indicate that the poet is here interested mainly in a sort of dramatic *tour de force* on what might have been a favourite theme of Sophistic debate rather than in making any moral point with regard to it. In *Hecuba*, on the other hand, the set speeches of Odysseus and of Hecuba, and their effectiveness in their respective contexts, do seem to suggest an uncomplimentary, though not perhaps a necessary, relation between rhetorical skill, or at least effectiveness, and moral probity.

V

Reality and Sense Perception

SOME SOPHISTIC VIEWS

Thus far we have been concerned with reasonably serious treatments by Euripides of themes suggested by the teachings of the Sophists. The next topic which we shall consider, viz. Sophistic views on man's perception of reality and on the communicability of these perceptions, became (or so we shall argue) the subject of parody in at least one of the extant plays of our dramatist.

Protagoras' famous *dictum*, 'Man is the measure of all things ...' has been the subject of much controversy which (fortunately) need not, for our present purposes, be resolved. One or two of its more obvious ambiguities should, however, be considered, for they may well have been ambiguities with which the philosopher's contemporaries, including Euripides, were faced.

We may begin with Plato's formulation of the doctrine at *Cratylus* 385Eff. (D-K 80 A13):

> Just as Protagoras declared saying that man is the measure of all things, that is, however things appear to me to be (*hoia men an emoi phainêtai*), so they *are* for me, and however things appear to be to you, so they *are* for you.

Plato gives the same description of Protagoras' doctrine at

Theaetetus 151Eff. (D-K 80 B1), except that he adds the example of wind, the coldness of which will be perceived differently by different persons, and concludes that for Protagoras 'appearance' and 'perception' (*phantasia* and *aisthêsis*), the basis, for each person, of 'being', are the same thing.

So far, then, it would seem that for Protagoras, 'reality' or 'truth' is completely relative to the individual perceiving it, and indeed that *that* 'reality' or 'truth' exists *only* for the individual perceiving it.

The much later authority Sextus (third century AD), however, expresses Protagoras' teaching somewhat differently. He begins:

> And Protagoras wishes man to be the measure of all things, of things that are (*tôn men ontôn*), that they are, and of things that are not, that they are not ... and for this reason he posits only what appears to the individual, thus introducing relativity (*eisagei to ti*).
>
> (Sextus, *Pyrrh. h.* I.216ff. = D-K 80 A14; cf. also B1)

However, Sextus qualifies this impression that man (whether 'man in general' or 'a particular man') is the sole determinant of appearances by adding, as a further Protagorean doctrine, that 'matter is in a state of flux' (*tên hulên rheustên einai*, 218), and, therefore, that the changes in what is perceived are due both to this and to the changes in man himself, depending on differences of age and other circumstances.

It is these discrepancies between Plato's and Sextus' accounts (and, for that matter, *within* Sextus' account) that have given rise to different views of Protagoras' teaching about sense-perception and reality.[1] Nevertheless, Guthrie seems justified in rejecting Sextus' 'qualification' of Plato's formulation of Protagoras' view, on the basis of Aristotle's evidence at *Metaph.* 1047a4-7:

> ... there is nothing [according to this argument] either hot or cold or sweet or perceptible in any way, if there is no one perceiving it, and so they [i.e. those who hold this view] must agree with the teaching of Protagoras.

Thus Guthrie concludes (p. 186):

> ... Protagoras adopted an extreme subjectivism according to which there was no reality behind and independent of appearances, no difference between appearing and being, and we are each the judge of our own impressions.

The primacy of an individual's sense perception as, for him, the only source of reality may well have been accepted by other Sophists as well as Protagoras. The author of the *Dissoi Logoi* (which show much Protagorean influence) would probably have subscribed to this doctrine. It could, at any rate, have been used among several of the examples which this author gives of his claim (D-K 90.4) that a statement may be true or false depending on the circumstances and the speaker. Gorgias, however, seems not always to have done so, for in his work on Nature he established, at least to his own satisfaction if not to Aristotle's (as Diogenes quotes him at v. 25, cited at D-K 82 B3, *ad fin.*), that nothing exists, but if anything *does* exist, it cannot be apprehended and that, if apprehensible, it cannot be expressed (see D-K 82 B3, *ad init.*). (On the other hand, it is possible that Gorgias is here indulging in a sort of logical exercise and that he held views on sense perception quite separate from those cited from his work on Nature. According to a passage in Plato's *Meno*, he seems to have followed Empedocles' explanation of sensation as effected by 'effluences' from the object. See Plato, *Meno* 76Cff. [D-K 82 B4]. With the first two of these propositions (and proofs) of Gorgias about 'the existent' we are not here concerned. The argument for the third, however, is interesting for comparison and contrast with other contemporary views on the relation between external reality and human understanding, or the communicability of that understanding. Here Gorgias asserts his proposition, namely that the existent cannot be communicated, by distinguishing existing things (*ta onta*), which are external reality (*haper ektos hupokeitai*), from the *logos*, or verbal account, by which such communication would have to be effected.

> For [Gorgias argues] that by which we reveal is *logos* but *logos* is not substances and existing things (*ta hupokeimena kai onta*) (D-K 82 B3, section 84; for the argument as a whole, see sections 83-6).

More significant than Gorgias' denial of the effectiveness of *logoi* as an instrument for the communication of reality was the Sophistic teaching that only one term or 'name' (*onoma*) might be used to describe any one entity.[2] This doctrine was associated particularly with Prodicus, though it was by no means restricted to his teaching. (See D-K 84 A14-18; the sources are various Platonic dialogues; in the quotation in A17 [from *Laches* 197D], Prodicus is said, most of all the Sophists, to make these excessive distinctions in applying names.) In D-K 84 A19, a quotation from Aristotle (*Topics* II.6, 112b22) criticizes Prodicus for seeking to distinguish kinds of pleasure by allotting a different name (*onoma*) to each.

Perhaps the best description of this doctrine of *onomatôn orthotês*, or 'rightness of names', occurs at Plato, *Cratylus* 383A-B (in a statement attributed to Cratylus):

> Everything has a right name of its own which comes by nature, and a name is not whatever people call a thing by agreement ... but there is a kind of constituted correctness in names which is the same for all men, both Greeks and barbarians.[3]

These assorted Sophistic teachings on 'sense perception and reality', and on the communicability of our experience of reality, are not all strictly compatible in philosophic terms. However, as we shall see, this possible lack of philosophic compatability between the accounts will be of no great importance for the purposes for which we have set them down.

APPEARANCE AND REALITY IN *HELEN*

Of the extant plays of Euripides, it is *Helen* which provides the most brilliant parody of the theme of 'appearance and reality' and of the various Sophistic teachings associated with it. A brief summary of the plot of *Helen* will provide an initial indication of how the poet deploys this theme.[4]

According to Euripides' version of the Helen myth (a fanciful development of Stesichorus' lost palinode on Helen),[5] Helen never went to Troy at all. Instead, Hera, to spite Aphrodite, caused a convincing wraith to accompany Paris to Troy, while the real Helen was delivered by Hermes to King Proteus of Egypt, thence to be restored (so the gods planned) to Menelaus when the Trojan War should be over. Thus the Trojan War was fought for a wraith, but one substantial enough, apparently, to deceive Paris, and later

Menelaus, when he rescues her from Troy. Meanwhile, the good King Proteus has died and Helen languishes near his tomb, seeking sanctuary from the wicked designs of his successor, Theoclymenus, who has sworn death to any Greek, and especially Menelaus, who might approach his shores. Thus the stage is set for a comedy of mistaken identity (Helen and her wraith), of false reputation (for Helen, much maligned among the Greeks, is actually as chaste as Penelope), and various other plays on the 'appearance/reality' theme.

The first of these occurs (68ff.) with the arrival of Teucer (almost accidentally: dramatic probability is not a prominent feature of this play), who is amazed to see someone so like Helen but who rejects the (present) evidence of his senses since he has seen 'the real Helen' being dragged away from Troy by Menelaus.

This Prologue scene is, however, only an anticipation of its more significant doublet, the Recognition scene (which is almost a Recognition *manqué*), between Helen and Menelaus. Menelaus, entering as a shipwrecked sailor in rags but giving 'a second Prologue speech', full of grandiloquence about his heroic past, provides a theatrical illustration of the 'appearance/reality' contrast which this scene is to develop. Once again, which is the appearance, which the reality? There is, of course, no doubt in Menelaus' mind: he, along with Agamemnon, formed that 'renowned yoke' (*kleinon zeugon*, 392, a nice Aeschylean imitation) which conquered Troy. However, when the heroic Menelaus is unceremoniously chased from the palace gates by an Old Portress, one is not so sure. The perplexities of the coming Recognition scene are now introduced by the Portress's information that one Helen of Sparta, 'daughter of Zeus', 'Tyndareus' child' (470, 472) resides within the palace and that the Egyptian King promises death to any Greek rival who might approach his shores.

For a moment Menelaus is shaken by this triple identification (by name, home and parentage) of the wife he *knows* he has left back in the cave near his wrecked ship. However, a brief reflection (497-9) on 'nominal plurality' ('for many men have the same name in many a land, and so with cities and women, too!') reassures him – until Helen herself appears and the Recognition scene proper is ready to begin. After her initial fright at Menelaus' unheroic appearance, Helen accepts her husband's self-identification (she is expecting him: she has been assured of his survival from shipwreck by Theonoe, the pious and clairvoyant priestess sister of the wicked Egyptian King). Menelaus, however, continues to believe in the wraith he has rescued from Troy. The highly comic scene in which he resists the evidence of his senses and the embraces of his eager wife, is finally resolved by a novel version of the conventional moment of revelation or 'discovery': the news, brought by a sailor from the scene of the wreck, that the wraith has disappeared into the heavens, confessing all as it ascends (605ff.).

The mistaken identity motif is continued (again amusingly) in the successfully executed *mêchanêma* or 'escape plot' (1193-1300). (The intervening scene, in which the complicity of Theonoe is secured, need not detain us here.) Menelaus, following up a lying tale told to Theoclymenus by Helen that 'Menelaus' has drowned at sea, plays the role of a shipwrecked Greek sailor, presides over his own funeral rites, fully equipped by a grateful Theoclymenus (now promised Helen as his wife) with ship, crew, arms and provisions – all that is needed for the escape across the seas. Thus we may say that the 'appearance and reality' theme is continued, though not perhaps as vividly as in the first half of the play, with the imaginary corpse of the (allegedly) drowned Menelaus replacing the (now vanished) wraith of Helen.

The ambiguity which we have observed throughout *Helen* between 'what is' and 'what is not' reaches beyond matters of identity to include even the person and reputation of Helen herself: her beauty, which appears to be an asset but which (as she has experienced it) is not (27 and 261ff.), and her character, which *seems* to her fellow Greeks to be disreputable but actually is not (270).

I have suggested that these elaborate plays, in *Helen*, on the 'appearance and reality' theme are intended as a parody of Sophistic teachings on these matters, particularly, perhaps, of the Sophists' insistence on the primacy of individual sense perceptions as criteria of truth, or 'reality', and on the use of names (*onomata*) and, indeed, on the dependability (or otherwise) of speech (*logos*) in the expression of that reality. A glance at the language by which the poet expresses the ambiguities on which we have commented may help to substantiate this claim.

The language for the deception and confusion which *appearances* may (and in the situation of the *Helen* do) provide begins in the Prologue, where several problematical concepts are introduced (though the speaker may not always be aware of them as such) which are to recur in various different contexts throughout the play. Thus, Helen describes her wraith as 'a mere seeming', 'an empty *dokêsis*, – and yet Paris thinks he has me, though not having me at all' (35-6). (According to Protagoras, as we have seen [D-K 80 A13 and B1, quoted above], Paris' sense perceptions of the wraith as *Helen* would presumably be true for him.) Here the verb *dokei* (which can, as here, mean 'he seems' as well as 'he thinks') is used in connection with *dokêsis*, the word by which Helen reminds us that the wraith is only 'a seeming'. However, not only Paris is deceived. The wraith becomes the cause of the Trojan War: 'Not I, but my name (*onoma*),' explains Helen, introducing, as she does so, another concept relevant to our theme, 'was set forth as the prize of the Trojan War' (42-3).

The emphasis on the uncertainty of relying on sense perceptions reappears with the entry of Teucer, but now it is Helen herself who, in Teucer's words, is the *likeness* (*eikos*) of Helen. Indeed, Teucer's utterances at 72-7 and 80 provide the best examples of the ambiguities and uncertainties which are to underlie sense perceptions throughout the play. Teucer, until he remembers his manners ('I yielded more to anger than I should have!', 80), is ready to slay Helen because of this likeness (as he thinks) to Helen. Thus his own vision, or 'seeing' (*opsis*, 72), on which he depends implicitly, deceives him, just as we learn, from his answers to Helen's questions, it deceived him at Troy:

Helen: Did you actually *see* (*eides*) the wretched woman? Or do you speak from hearsay?
Teucer: As plainly as I see you, with my own eyes. And the mind sees (*kai nous horâi*)![6]

(*Hel.* 121-2)

Both the key terms and the (in my view) Sophistic doctrines, which we have noted in the two Prologue scenes, recur, in a new form, in the first episode. The question of names occurs in Menelaus' prologue to his first scene with Helen, where we have heard that hero blithely contradicting Prodicus in advance as he reassures himself (at 497ff.), despite the identical names, on the 'otherness' from *his* Helen of this local Helen residing in the Egyptian palace. Menelaus becomes more orthodox later in this speech, when he asserts that no one can fail to recognize *his* name as that of the famous conqueror of Troy:

For no one is so barbarous of mind as not to give me

> food, when he hears *my* name. Famous is the fire of Troy and famous I who kindled it – I, Menelaus, not unknown in *any* land! (*Hel.* 501-4)

In the 'failed Recognition scene' between Helen and Menelaus, we find the same emphasis as in the Teucer scene on words for seeing and on the delusions of sight. '... What vision, woman, do I see in you?' (*tin' opsin sên, gunai, prosderchomai;*) cries Menelaus (at 557) when he first sees Helen. A little later he suspects, as presumably Protagoras would, that if his senses are ill so his mind must be (*ou pou phronô men eu, to d' omma mou nosei*; 'Is my mind failing then, in that my eye is sick?', 575). Helen, now desperate to be recognized, insists, 'What else can inform you other than your eyes?' (580), though she has, a few minutes earlier, warned Teucer *against* such evidence (at 119 and 121) when Teucer declared that he had seen Helen at Troy 'with my own eyes' (118 and 122). Exasperated, Menelaus introduces a new Sophistic ploy ('deeds over words!') in refutation of Helen's claims: 'The greatness of my labours (*ponoi*) over there [i.e. at Troy] persuades me; you do not!' (593).

Two of the verbal (Sophistic?) antitheses which we have noted in this scene are repeated in a somewhat different context in the Messenger speech which brings the Recognition scene to a close. Describing what he is about to tell as 'wondrous things' (*thaumasta*, 601), the Messenger declares this term (*onoma*) to be less wondrous than the event (*pragma*) itself.[7] And after completing his tale, the Messenger, in his summing up, reminds us of Menelaus' own concluding argument to Helen when he compares Helen's troubles from words of ill report to Menelaus' labours with the spear (717).

Words for misleading sense perceptions and antithetical terms, such as *onoma*, *pragma* and the like, are not, however, the only sources of ambiguity and delusion in the play. *Logos* ('word', 'speech', 'report'), its cognates and, occasionally, synonymous expressions, also occur with significant frequency throughout.

In the first half of the play, *logos* and its synonyms are associated particularly with beliefs or myths of which the truth is somehow doubted by the speaker. Good examples of this are to be found in Helen's sceptical expressions about tales of her mythical conception: 'There is a certain story' (*estin de ... logos tis*), 17ff., and 'if this tale be true' (*ei saphês houtos logos*), 21; a similar expression occurs in Helen's account of her strange birth from an egg: 'so they say' (*phasin*).[8] And we have seen, too, Menelaus' reservations (at 593) about the truth of Helen's tale of the wraith in comparision with the *labours* which *he* underwent at Troy. Teucer also sometimes uses words for 'story' or 'speech' dismissively of their truth (though he is not, of course, always right!): once, concerning Helen's warning that what he saw at Troy may have been an illusion ('Think of some other story' (*logou*)!, 120); once, when he mentions two reports (*duo logô*, 138) about Helen's brothers, only one of which he clearly regards as true.

In the second half of the play, through the gulling of Theoclymenus by Helen and Menelaus, outright deception replaces the illusions of false sense perceptions, the allegedly drowned body of Menelaus corresponding, in a sense, to the wraith of Helen. 'Speech words' now replace words for 'seeming' and the like, such as *dokei*, *dokêsis,* in this new context of deception. It is true that in this context it would be difficult to avoid such words entirely. However, it is equally difficult to believe that their repeated use in certain passages is not intended to draw attention to the potentialities of speech for the purpose of delusion and falsification. Consider, for example, Helen's persuasion of Menelaus to conspire in the bold plan for deceiving Theoclymenus:

> Are you willing, though not having died, to have done so by report? (*boulei legesthai me thanôn logôi thanein;*)
> (*Hel.* 1050)

To which Menelaus replies:

> ... if by so saying I win gain, then I am ready, though not having died, to have done so by report (*me thanôn logôi thanein*). (*Hel.* 1051-2)

Here the redundancy of *legesthai* ... *logôi*, repeated almost verbatim in Menelaus' reply (the jingle is more effective in the Greek than in translation), tends to underline the deceptive function of *logos*.[9]

In the first half of the play, then, we have seen both Helen's doubts about stories of her conception and birth and her own difficulties in seeking, by words, to explain to Teucer and Menelaus the illusions created by the wraith, i.e. the distinction, in this case, between illusion and reality. In the escape *mêchanêma*, on the other hand, we see Helen (and, when instructed, Menelaus) using words for the persuasion and deception of Theoclymenus. We may remember, perhaps, Gorgias' two rather different views of words (*logoi*), expressed in different contexts: first, the view that words are incapable of expressing reality (D-K 82 B3, 84), and second, the successful use of words in deceptive persuasions (D-K 82 B11, in *The Encomium of Helen*) especially section 8:

> If it was speech (*logos*) that persuaded her [Helen] and deceived her soul, then it is not difficult to defend her

> and to free her from blame. Speech is a great power which accomplishes the most marvellous effects by the smallest and least visible means ...

Is it a critical extravagance to imagine that Euripides, in the two 'action sequences' of the *Helen*, is reflecting first the one and then the other of Gorgias' two reported views of *logos*?

Before ending our discussion of the *Helen*, however, we should return briefly to what I believe to be the main thrust of the poet's treatment of Sophistic themes in this play. The strange *jeu d'esprit* on the 'appearance and reality' theme, though it is most prominent in the first panel of the play, informs the whole work. Does it have a latent tragic meaning? If so, I believe that it may be expressed, though still in ambiguous terms, in the first stasimon (1107-64), which occurs between Helen's formulation of her escape plan and its successful execution.

This ode reflects, in mournful and philosophic strain, on the seemingly unnecessary woes of Trojans and Greeks alike in the Trojan War. In the first strophe, the initial cause of those woes, Paris' abduction of Helen, is described in almost brutally literal terms:

> ... when Paris, the ill-starred bridegroom (*Paris ainogamos*), came ... bringing you from Lacedaimon O Helen, as his bed-mate (*lechea/sethen*, 1119-20, [*lit.*, 'a bed-mate consisting of you']), a marriage full of woe for the sons of Priam.[10] (*Hel.* 1117-21)

Certainly there is no hint here of wraiths or illusions.

In the corresponding antistrophe (1132-6), on the other hand, Menelaus' rescue of Helen (*Menelaus* is subject of *esuto*,

1133; see Dale's note *ad loc.*) is described in very different terms. Helen is now 'no prize but a cause of strife' (*geras ou geras, all'erin*, 1134), and is called a 'divine (or cursed?) likeness formed by Hera' (*eidôlon hieron Hêras*, 1136).

The full purpose of the two versions (first the actual, then the illusory) of the rape of Helen, in the first strophe of this ode, becomes clear in its final antistrophe, 1151-64. Here the Chorus inveighs against all those who hope to end men's struggles (*ponous thnatôn*, 1153-4) by contests of blood, for in that case 'strife (*eris*, 1156) will never leave the cities of men' (1156-7). And now it is 'strife over Helen', the Chorus concludes, which has caused both the destruction of Troy and the deaths of many Greeks (see 1158-64).

In this last passage we should note particularly the expression 'strife over you, O Helen' (*san erin, O Helena*) at 1160, which repeats *eris* at 1156, and also at 1134 in the first antistrophe, where it has been used synonymously with Hera's wraith, *eidôlon hieron Hêras*, 1136. In the *action* of the play, the cause of the Trojan War has been expressed as an illusion caused by the gods. Now, in the final antistrophe of this ode, this illusion is allowed to symbolize, for a moment, all the illusions which the poet believes to be the causes of wars.

VI

Nomos and Related Ideas

NOMOS AND *PHUSIS* AMONG THE SOPHISTS

An interest in *nomos*, and in various ideas and discussions related to it, is one of the best known features of Sophistic thought. This is, of course, not surprising: much of the professional activity of the Sophists was concerned with teaching young men how to become good and successful citizens; it was as a background to this teaching that the Sophists developed their theories and myths about the origins of civilized society, and the introduction of law was, of course, an essential feature of such theories. Our direct evidence of this is, as with all Sophistic teaching, very limited, and must, as often, be supplemented by the very qualified evidence of Plato's dialogues.

Guthrie has well described the two uses of *nomos* among 'the Sophists, historians and orators of the day (and ... [by] the tragedian Euripides, another spokesman of the new thought)' as:

> (i) usage or custom, based on traditional beliefs, as to what is right or true, (ii) laws formally drawn up and passed which codify 'right usage' and elevate it into an obligatory norm backed by the authority of the state. The first was the earlier use, but was never lost sight of,

> so that for the Greeks law, however much it might be formulated in writing and enforced by authority, remained dependent on custom or habit.[1]

Let us consider first one or two Sophistic views, or at least theories, concerning the origin of law.

In a passage quoted earlier[2] from Critias (D-K 88 B25), we have already seen the view that 'a certain wise man discovered fear of the gods' as a means of making men obey the laws, even when they had no witnesses. In the same passage it is made quite clear that the laws themselves were invented by man as a means of rescuing men from their brutish lives in which violence predominated. A comparable, though more 'philosophical' account (with an interesting difference) is attributed to Protagoras, in his 'myth of Prometheus', by Plato (*Prt.* 320C-322D). According to Protagoras' account, men, though provided, through Prometheus' thefts of fire and the practical arts, with the basic means of survival, were unable to live peacefully together in communities until Zeus sent Hermes with the gifts of *aidôs* (respect) and *dikê* (justice); he further instructed Hermes to establish the law (*nomos*) that anyone incapable of acquiring these virtues should be put to death.

While it is the gods who, in the myth of Prometheus. establish the law, it is clear that in *both* Sophistic versions it is law which is regarded as the basis of civilized or community existence. This emphasis and the relatively secondary importance of religious belief which may or may not be involved is relevant, as we shall see, to the treatment in certain Euripidean tragedies of civilized relations between states, or of the tribal forerunners of states in mythical times. (That the teachings of the historical Protagoras precede the writings of Critias does not matter for our discussions. Both the latter and Plato's versions of the former presumably represent the sort of things which were said about 'law' and 'the laws' by the Sophists, and this is what we are concerned with in discussing Euripides' dramatic deployment of such ideas. And indeed the element of similarity between the passages cited from Critias and from Plato's *Protagoras* helps to support at least this degree of historical validity for the idea expressed in mythical form by Plato's Protagoras).

Another important part of Sophistic discussons of 'law' and 'the laws' involved the distinction, and the conflicting claims, between *nomos* and *phusis*, *phusis* connoting 'external reality', 'the way things are', *nomos*, the restrictions, prescriptions and the like imposed by convention or legislation. This distinction was not, of course, new. However, by the mid-fifth century, philosophers began to emphasize the antithesis as it affected human conduct and attitudes. The earliest certain extant reference to such a concern in this context occurs in a brief fragment from Archelaus (a scientific thinker of the mid-fifth century of whose ethical views little is known): 'The shameful is not "by nature" (*phusêi*) but "by convention" (*nomôi*)' (60A1). The same distinction made in more general terms occurs in a fragment attributed uncertainly to Hippocrates: 'Law and Nature (*nomos kai phusis*), though coming to terms with one another, do not agree' (Hippocrates D-K 42 C1). So also, a little later in the same fragment: 'Men set down laws (*nomous*), but the gods arranged the nature (*phusin*) of all things.'

Among attitudes attributed to the Sophists, we find a sharper contrast between the values attributed to *phusis* and *nomos*, respectively, in the celebrated declaration attributed by Socrates to Callicles, in Plato's *Gorgias*: 'That which is right by nature is superior to our laws' (*Gorgias* 482C4ff.). With this we may compare the similar assertion of Thrasymachus in the *Republic*: 'Justice is the rule of the strong' (*Republic* I.336ff.), though the terms *nomos* and *phusis* are not used. (We must remember, of course, as always in Plato's dialogues, that Socrates may well attribute positions, especially extreme positions, to the Sophists in the interest of the dialectical progression of his own (or more probably of Plato's own) argument; elsewhere, Thrasymachus is said to have written that justice was the greatest of all things among men (D-K 85 B8), a sentiment which hardly accords with the views attributed to him in *Republic* I).[3]

Among more verifiable views of the Sophists on the *nomos/phusis* controversy, the fragments of Antiphon provide the best (though sometimes rather puzzling) examples. (Some of the passages quoted below from Antiphon (D-K 87 B44) have already been discussed in another context – that of Sophistic views on the relativity of virtue.)[4]

Antiphon begins (87 B44) conventionally enough: 'Justice consists in not transgressing the laws of the city of which one is a citizen.' He goes on to say, however, that a man would follow justice most profitably for himself if he should obey the laws when he has witnesses, but the dictates of nature (*ta tês phuseôs*) when there are no witnesses, 'for the dictates of law are imposed (*epitheta*), while those of nature are necessary (*anagkaia*)'. Next, Antiphon compares offences against the laws with offences against nature, finding the latter to be an evil whether one escapes notice or not, 'for one is injured not because of men's opinion, but because of truth' (*ou gar dia doxan blaptetai, alla di' alêtheian*). Antiphon's arguments in favour of *phusis* seem to reach their apogee with the claim that many of the things that are just according to law (*tôn kata nomôn dikaiôn*) are hostile to nature (*polemious têi phusêi*). Antiphon concludes (after a complex argument not relevant to our purposes), that 'advantages derived from the laws are chains on nature'. Thus (since he has already shown that to offend nature is worse than to offend against the laws), Antiphon's preference for the claims of *phusis* over those of *nomos* seems (at least in *this* passage) to be fairly clearly established.

Antiphon's statements in the fragment just summarized provide the strongest (and most pragmatic!) 'ethical' defence of *phusis* which we find in the tradition on the Sophists. It is, of course, quite possible, as Kerferd has argued, that Antiphon is here expressing a view which he intends to assail, but this may, of course, be claimed of many fragmentary, and so incomplete, arguments in the pre-Socratic tradition. On the whole, it seems preferable to accept Antiphon's statements at face value, as representing his own views, though possibly expressed in extreme form for argumentative purposes. As Guthrie puts it, 'The general impression … is of a single writer determined to show up the inadequacy of current conceptions of morality.'[5]

The last of the Sophistic passages at which we should look is from the Anonymus Iamblichi, which can, perhaps, only marginally and tentatively be called Sophistic. Its author is thought to be a writer of the late fifth or early fourth century, possibly one influenced by Protagoras.[6] The passage relating to the *phusis/nomos* issue is of particular interest because, alone of the passages which we have considered, it suggests an essential relation between the two concepts which elsewhere have been regarded as antithetical. It runs as follows:

> If men were given such a nature that they were not able to live alone but formed an association with one another under pressure of necessity … and cannot live together without observance of law, … we can conclude, then, that because of these necessities Law and Justice are

> kings among men, and could in no way change, for by nature they have been firmly fixed (*phusêi gar ischura endedesthai tauta*).[7] (*Anon. Iamblichi*: D-K 89.6.1, in part; Reesor's translation).

NOMOS AND RELATED TERMS IN EURIPIDES' POLITICAL PLAYS

In a passage in Euripides' *Hecuba* which I have already quoted in my discussion of Sophistic views of the gods in Euripides,[8] Hecuba attributes not only belief in the gods but definitions of 'what is just and what is unjust' to *nomos*. In this passage (*Hec.* 799-801) the description of *nomos* appears in the captive Trojan Queen's appeal to Agamemnon for help in vengeance against Polymestor for his violation of the laws of hospitality in murdering Polydorus. 'Reverence me!' (*aidesthêti me*, 806) cries Hecuba, invoking that virtue (*aidôs*) which we have seen that the Platonic Protagoras described (at *Prt.* 322Cff.) as fundamental to civilized relations within the community.

The theme of *nomos* and the associated virtues of *aidôs* and *dikê* are not developed in *Hecuba*, but they play an important part in Euripides' two most political plays, *Supplices* (*The Suppliant Women*) and *Heraclidae* (*The Children of Heracles*). Both these plays concern the theme of supplication; in both Athens is involved in the championing of the weak against the strong. However, while *Supplices* idealizes *nomos* as a concept essential to the co-existence of civilized states, *Heraclidae* is more concerned with the virtues of *aidôs* and *dikê* in the defence of the weak against a stronger antagonist (a defence, in other words, of civilized justice against the claims of 'natural justice', as defined by the Thrasymachus and Callicles of the Platonic dialogues, and, though in more complex terms, by Antiphon).

Let us glance first at the treatment of these related themes in *Heraclidae.* Though less ambitious than the single-minded idealization of *nomos* in *Supplices*, it provides, perhaps, more vivid illustrations of the shifting attitudes (such as we might find them expressed in arguments of the Sophists) of individuals and states as they experience the vicissitudes of fortune.

Iolaus, in the opening lines (1-5) of *Heraclidae*, declares:

> Long have I held this to be true: the just man (*ho … dikaios*) lives for his friends and his associates, but the man whose spirit is given up to gain (*kerdos*) is both useless to the state (*polei*) and grievous to associate with but best for himself; not merely by report have I come to know this truth. (*Heracl.* 1-5)

David Lupher rightly observes that 'this general reflection … establishes the atmosphere of thought and feeling which will dominate this play …'.[9] Justice (*dikê*) and gain (*kerdos*), are to be the two poles around which the action of the play revolves. Iolaus, through his sense of justice and reverence for kin, has (as he tells us in the following verses) come to the aid of the children of Heracles, relentlessly pursued by the Argive King Eurystheus. His opponent, the Argive Herald Kopreus, will try (as we shall see) to persuade the Athenians to seek their own gain by joining the strong against the weak and abandoning the Heraclidae to the Argives.

The Chorus, confronting the Argive Herald (who has thrown old Iolaus to the ground) also declare their support for the Heraclidae in the name of justice (*dika*, 104) and reverence for the suppliant (*hiktêras aideisthai*, 101). Justice is, however, also invoked by Kopreus (143), in his first speech to Demophon, along with law (*nomos*, 141), on the grounds that the Argives have the right to fulfill their own edicts. His argument is later refuted by Iolaus (185-8). However, by this time the violent Herald has dropped this argument in favour of his more characteristic one: the promise of the gain or profit which Athens will achieve by supporting the stronger rather than the weaker side ('*ti kerdaneis;*' he asks the Athenian King, 154). Ironically, the argument based on *kerdos* is to be applied in the reverse direction, as it were, in the complex finale of the play. When the Argive King has been defeated and captured by the Athenians, Alcmene, the vengeful mother of the Heraclidae, persuades the Athenians to let her slay Eurystheus, but at least the Athenians secure from her the promise that she will return his corpse for burial at Athens. In his final speech, Eurystheus then promises as a reward (*kerdos*, 1043) to the Athenians that his bones will protect them against a future attack by the Heraclidae (i.e. the Spartans of a future generation).[10]

'Favour' or 'obligation', another ethical concept of ambiguous applicability, also plays its part in this drama of shifting loyalties. In his initial appeal for refuge against the threatened violence of the Argive Herald, Iolaus reminds King Demophon of the obligations which he owes to Heracles: in addition to the relationship of Demophon to the Heraclidae, Heracles himself had brought back Theseus (father of Demophon) from Hades:

> ... and he brought your father back from Hades' lowest keep. All of Greece bears witness to this deed. And for these obligations his children ask another favour back: that they should not be torn with violence from the gods' altars and cast forth from this land. (*Heracl.* 218-22)

We should note, in this passage, the terms *apaitousin ... antidounai ... charin*, which express the peculiarly Greek emphasis on reciprocity in Iolaus' appeal. When he has won King Demophon's protection, Iolaus then warns the Heraclidae, in turn, of the debt which *they* now owe to Athens, so that they must remember never to raise a hostile spear against her. In the play's finale, however, there is once again an ironic reminder of this undertaking by Iolaus for the Heraclidae, and an ironic shift in the application of favours promised for favours received. The defeated Eurystheus, once the opponent of the Athenians, now describes the prophesied attack of the descendants of the Heraclidae as a betrayal of the favour (*charin*, 1036) which they recived from the Athenians. Eurystheus himself, on the contrary, promises his protection (as we have seen) to the Athenians in reward for their burial of his body.

It will be clear even from this brief highlighting of the terms and concepts involved that several political and ethical ideas much discussed by the Sophists are germane to the issues of this play. Such terms as *aidôs* and *dikê* are used repeatedly in the context of allegedly civilized behaviour (indeed, *dikê* is used on opposite sides of the same argument). These are, as we have seen, the two virtues which, according to the Platonic Protagoras, are to be protected by law as necessary for the preservation of the civilized community. Lupher suggests that 'it is in the Prologue of this play that we first detect the accents of Protagoras'.[11]

So, too, the conflict presented in this play between the claims of the weaker suppliants and the claims of their more powerful adversaries reminds us of similar Sophistic debates between the claims of *nomos* and *phusis*. Iolaus makes this point both in his poignant account (23-5) of other peoples who have abandoned them to the stronger side and, most emphatically, in his praise of the Athenians:

> ... who, looking on us poor wanderers, have set us free and taken as *their* enemies that great host and land Pelasgian; wretched though we were, they still did not surrender us nor drive us from us from the land.
>
> (*Heracl.* 316-19)

Kopreus, on the other hand (150ff., 154ff.), points to the gain which Athens will acquire by joining the stronger (Argive) side, thus clearly aligning himself with the arguments of Antiphon, and the Platonic Callicles and Thrasymachus, in favour of the advantages of nature (*phusis*) over those of law (*nomos*).

As far as the theme of supplication in *Heraclidae* is concerned, Athens is certainly presented as the champion of the suppliant, and of the weaker against the stronger side. However, the intransigent attitude of Alcmene (mother of the Heraclidae) with regard to the Athenians' captive, Eurystheus, and certainly the future attack on Athens by the descendants of the Heraclidae (as foretold in prophecy related by Eurystheus), rather detract from the earlier assurances of undying obligation by Iolaus. Nothing, neither the observance of the traditional, unwritten laws governing kinship and favours owed, nor even the continued friendship of friends or enmity of enemies, seems able, in the action of this play, to be taken for granted. For this reason it can, perhaps, be described as one of Euripides' most Sophistic plays, both in its iconoclasm with regard to traditional values and certainties, and in its presentation of shifting attitudes and arguments suggestive of the more chameleonic aspects of Sophistic discourse. (I should add that *Heraclidae*, despite, or possibly because of, these interesting intellectual aspects, is not, in my opinion, a particularly effective tragedy.)

Little of this complexity attaches to the other Euripidean play (called, appropriately, *Supplices*) dealing with the theme of supplication. Nevertheless, *Supplices* may also be said to provide, though in much more positive tone, a celebration of a Sophistic theme: the idealization of *nomos*, which, as I have suggested at the beginning of this Chapter, was a concept fundamental to the more positive aspects of Sophistic thought and teaching.

In *Supplices*, the Argive King Adrastus appeals to Theseus of Athens on behalf of the mothers of the slain Argive heroes (the Chorus in the play) to persuade the Thebans, by force if necessary, to allow them to bury the bodies of their sons. First, in Theseus' initial speech of refusal to Adrastus, and later in his acceptance of the Suppliants' plea, this play, more than any other Euripidean play, develops in two separate contexts the themes of 'the well-ordered society' and of its necessary preservation, by means of law, throughout the Hellenic world.

Preliminary notes of the *nomos*-theme are heard in Aithra's Prologue account of the situation, where the Thebans' refusal of burial of the slain warriors is described as 'dishonouring the laws of the gods' (*nomim' atizontes theôn*, 19) and is repeated by the Chorus' appeal at 378, '... lest they pollute the laws (*nomous*) of men'. However, development of this theme is postponed until after Theseus' initial rejection of Adrastus' appeal on behalf of the suppliant mothers. This rejection takes the curious form of an account (195ff.) of 'the well-ordered life' which man enjoys, thanks to the benevolence of some (unnamed) god, but which Adrastus has sacrificed for his community by throwing in his lot with accursed stock.[12] It is for Adrastus' contemning of the divinely bestowed 'good life' – and particularly of the gift of divination, by which he might have been warned against his dangerous course of action (211ff., cf. 155ff.) – that Theseus rejects Adrastus' plea.

Theseus' account (195ff.) of the well-ordered life on which Adrastus has unwisely turned his back follows a form similar (at least in most of its features) to the evolutionary accounts of the origins of civilized society which had become common in the Sophistic period and even before it.[13]

> With other men, indeed, have I laboured in arguments along these lines: for one man has said that there are more bad things in life than good, but *I* hold the opposite view that the good things outnumber the evil ones for mortals. For if this were not the case, we would not be in the light of day. And I praise whichever of the gods it was who bestowed order on our life, lifting it out of a confused and brutish state. First, he gave us intelligence, then speech, words' messengers, so that we might understand discourse; then nourishment by fruit, and drops of rain by which the god might foster what the earth brings forth and provide water for man's thirst as well; then he, this god, also gave us protections against the winter's cold and summer heat; then he provided crossings of the sea by ships so that we might have commerce with others for what our land might lack. And whatever is obscure or which we do not clearly understand, prophets foretell by gazing into the fire or by means of folds of sacrificial innards and by the flight of birds. (*Suppl.* 195-213)

(It is Adrastus' neglect of this gift of augury in favour of

Delphic prophecy (214ff.) that is the particular cause of Theseus' criticism.)

There are several curious features of this part of Theseus' speech. One is its questionable relevance to Theseus' rejection of Adrastus. Another is the omission of several typical features of such evolutionary accounts, such as an emphasis on the *successive* fulfilment of human needs as the connection between the series of improvements to living and a corresponding emphasis on human ingenuity. Most of all, perhaps, one misses the expected culmination of this civilizing sequence, the achievement (with the aid of *nomos* and associated virtues) of communal living in the *polis*. Just as one recognizes that Theseus' initial rejection of the suppliants can only be a stage, a necessary 'complication', in the plot, so, too, one realizes that a part of the development of the theme of 'the well-ordered society' must await Theseus' later acceptance of the Suppliants' plea and the reasons he gives for that acceptance.[14]

It is Aithra's speech of advice (at 300ff.) to her son Theseus which prompts Theseus' second response to Adrastus' supplication. Aithra begins by firmly reminding Theseus that he must not neglect the gods' concerns (*ta tôn theôn*, 301) and that it is a matter of duty to be valorous on behalf of those being unjustly treated. Aithra adds significantly that it will bring Theseus honour to stop those who were destroying the accepted practices of all Greece (*nomima ... pasês ... Hellados*, 311) by preventing the burial of the dead. Aithra further affirms that it is this which keeps cities together, whenever one keeps safe the laws (*hotan tis tous nomous sôizêi kalôs*, 313). As Collard has well observed: 'The obligation to bury the dead now appears for the first time [in the play] as panhellenic law ... and after his capitulation to Aithra, Theseus takes over the idea: 526, 621, ... 538.'[15] Thus Aithra has begun her speech with a reminder to Theseus not to neglect the gods' concerns, but she soon switches to an emphasis on political and social advantage. Theseus, on the other hand, in his speech to Adrastus, has indulged initially in an account of 'the good life' reminiscent of Sophistic humanism but has ended it with a rebuke to the Argive King for contemning the gifts of the god. Perhaps this paradox reflects the ambiguity which we have noted in Sophistic arguments about the priority of the gods or of *nomos* in establishing and preserving civilized society – or, indeed, about which of these two concepts is dependent on the other. However this may be, it is clear that both elements are given some prominence in the dramatic situation as it is presented so far.

Theseus' acceptance of his mother's advice in his speech at 334ff. is based on the same (typically Athenian) considerations of reputation and righteousness:

> ... to flee dangers accords not with my character, for I have always shown this nature (*ethos*) to the Greeks: always to be the scourge of wickedness.
>
> (*Suppl.* 339-41)

With the arrival of the Theban Herald, spokesman for tyranny, and the debate with Theseus which ensues, *nomos* is celebrated (by Theseus) in the context first of domestic, then of international politics. Against the Herald's claim for the advantages of one-man rule, Theseus advances the advantages *for the people*, of democratic, written laws:

> When laws are not possessed in common (*ouk eisi nomoi/ koinoi*), but one man for his own self-interest possesses law, then there is no equality. But when there are

written laws (*gegrammenôn de tôn nomôn*) then poor and rich have equal justice ... (*Suppl.* 430-4).

Here as elsewhere, *nomos* appears in close association with *dikê* (justice); see, for example, 437: 'The weaker one defeats the strong, when he has justice', where *dikaia echôn* seems almost equivalent to saying 'when he has law on his side'.

This same association of *nomos* and *dikê* is repeated in an international context in Theseus' final insistence to the Herald on his right to restore the bodies of the Argives to their grieving mothers for burial:

> I claim it just (*dikaiô*) to bury [them], preserving the law of all the Greeks (*ton panellênôn nomon*). (*Suppl.* 526-7)

This claim is repeated at 538 (*pasês Hellados koinon tode*) and finally in Theseus' ringing declaration at 561-3:

> Never will it be broadcast to the Greeks that when to me and Athens challenge came the ancient law of the gods (*nomos palaios daimonôn*) was then destroyed.

We see now why the dramatist has omitted *nomos* (and the *polis*) from Theseus' earlier 'evolutionary' account of the good life. Mention of this crowning and necessary achievement of communal living (as we have seen it in the *Protagoras*) has been saved for Athens' claim to protect not only the *polis* but all the civilized Greek community.

As we have noted in the speeches of Theseus and Aithra, 'the good life' and its protection have been presented sometimes in secular, sometimes in religious (or at least mythical) terms. This Sophistic ambiguity (as we have ventured to style it) is now continued in the iambic passage which follows between the two halves of the Chorus. One of these hemichoruses is optimistic and believes in just gods who distribute human happenings (614-17); here we should note *nemousi* (of the same root as *nomos*) at 612 at 617, in a context of 'just distributions' by the gods. The other, pessimistic hemichorus appears to doubt just gods (*dikaious daimonous*) at 610 and 612.

Thus (to recapitulate) the chief dramatic developments of Sophistic ideas which we have found in *Supplices* would seem to be the following: the emphasis in Theseus' decisive speeches on the evolution of civilized society and of the necessity of *nomos* for its preservation (here the extension of this view to the preservation of the Greek community as a whole may be a Euripidean formulation); the persistent ambiguity concerning 'the secular' and 'the sacred' view of the authority of *nomos*; and, finally, the prime application of this view to the defence of suppliants, which we have already found to be so prominent in *Heraclidae*, as a sort of link between the traditional laws of the gods (*nomos palaios daimonôn*, 563) and their more sophisticated 'modern' version in written laws (*gegrammenôn de tôn nomôn*, 433).

NOMOS AND *PHUSIS* IN *BACCHAE*

Bacchae is a play replete with paradoxes. Of these, perhaps the one most central to the play's meaning is that which seeks to bridge the gap between those apparently antithetical concepts, *nomos* and *phusis*. It would be surprising, in view of what we have observed in other Euripidean plays, if this treatment were not in some way related to the considerable Sophistic interest which we have noted in these matters.

Another almost equally striking paradox in *Bacchae* involves the distinction between 'wisdom' and 'cleverness', an issue on which the Sophists themselves would seem to have been somewhat vulnerable.

Dionysus in *Bacchae* is a new god, bringing a new religion to Thebes, to the city which has denied his divinity from his birth and whose young King, Pentheus, also rejects the strange and mystical cult which his followers profess. The newness of the god is stressed once, sarcastically, by Pentheus ('this *new* god [*tôn neôsti daimona*], Dionysus, whoever he is', 219) and once by his defender, Teiresias (*ho daimôn, ho neos*, 273). And the wildness of the god's cult, its life according to nature, is also stressed (though not always in a threatening context) by songs of the maenad Chorus and by the reports about the Theban women whom Dionysus has driven mad in the hills of Cithaeron.

Pentheus is presented as the puritanical ruler, insistent on law and order, who seeks to suppress the orgiastic cult of this imposter (as he believes Dionysus to be). Yet despite the newness of the god, and the ecstatic condition of his followers, we shall hear the Chorus claim that *their* way is the way that the *nomoi* from time immemorial dictate and that it is Pentheus, a wise fool, who lacks the true wisdom by which alone man can be saved. It is a measure of Euripides' dramatic and poetic power that he succeeds in convincing us of the Chorus' paradoxical claim.

While it is Dionysus disguised as his own priest who provides the dramatic contest with Pentheus, and brings to its tragic fulfilment the outcome of Pentheus' blind folly, it is the Chorus which expresses in a series of powerful odes the deeper meanings of Dionysianism. While Dionysus has given us a brief statement of his own history and present intentions, it is the parodos, a sort of cult hymn (as Dodds has described it) which provides the mythical and ritualistic background of Dionysian worship. Here one is struck (in view of the relative youthfulness of the god himself) by some of the more ancient associations and connections which the Chorus claims for the cult: the orgiastic rituals of Cybele (78ff.), for example, and the kettle-drums which once shielded the birth of the Cretan Zeus (121ff.). In a sense the choral odes are timeless, in a way that the action of the play can never be. By these associations with ancient chthonic cults in distant lands, a tradition is created for the new religion and a wider dimension of meaning. And it is this sense of an established tradition which, as we shall see, is to be essential to its claims. A hint of this part of the poet's purpose is given in the ritual cries in the prelude to the parodos (*tis hodôi; tis hodôi; tis; melathrois ektopos estô* ..., 68ff.) and in the declaration which follows these cries:

> For we shall always sing the traditional hymns (*ta nomisthenta*) in honour of Dionysus! (*Bacch.* 71).

(I am not suggesting, of course, that Dionysianism did not *have* these connections with ancient, chthonic cults; rather, that the Olympian and Theban Dionysian myth which provides the literal level of the dramatic action needs assistance of the kind indicated in establishing such associations.)

The Chorus' establishment of an instant tradition for the new god is greatly assisted by a statement from Teiresias near the beginning of the episode which follows this cult hymn to Dionysus. Cadmus and Teiresias, the only Thebans who have willingly accepted Dionysus and the new religion, are preparing to join the maddened Theban women in Bacchic rituals on Mt. Cithaeron. Cadmus has twice (179, 186) called Teiresias 'wise' (*sophos*) – the poet's way, perhaps, of alerting us to the importance of anything the prophet has to say. Teiresias gently qualifies Cadmus' compliment:

We are in no way wise in divine matters. Ancestral traditions (*patrious paradochas*) which we have received co-eval with time itself, no argument will overthrow (*katabalei*), not even if cleverness (*to sophon*) has been discovered by subtle wits. (*Bacch.* 200-2)

This is the only *dramatic* passage in the play which echoes the Chorus' constant celebration of the Dionysian cult as, in a sense, timeless, affecting (to put it in mythological terms) that part of man's nature which he shares with the divine. It is fitting that this should be expressed by the 'timeless' personage of Teiresias.[16]

From what has been said so far we may see, perhaps, how the association of the wild, enthusiastic 'new religion' with *nomos*, that which is regarded as traditionally acceptable, even conventional, is gradually established in the play. So it is that Cadmus (after Teiresias' rationalistic and perhaps Sophistic account of the 'real' meaning of Dionysus),[17] urges Pentheus to 'stay with us' (i.e. with Teiresias and himself) and not to 'venture beyond what custom allows' (*mê thuraze tôn nomôn*, 331). Otherwise, if unprepared for, this would surely seem a surprising warning concerning Pentheus' severity toward the new, barbaric cult.

Indeed the association between the Dionysian way of life and *nomos*, what is conventionally accepted by the common man, gradually becomes a regular feature of the Chorus' criticisms of 'the too clever ones', the unbelievers like Pentheus. Thus, in the first stasimon, after a rebuke to Pentheus' lawless (*anomos*) frenzy, the Chorus praises the Dionysian 'life of peacefulness and unshaken good sense (*to phronein asaleuton*), as what 'holds homes together' (389-92). This in turn leads to the Chorus' recurrent theme that 'cleverness [such as Pentheus' agnosticism] is not wisdom (*to sophon d' ou sophia*) and that to pursue more than mortal thoughts is not wisdom' (395-6). At the end of this ode, the Chorus sums up the contrast (a sinister one for Pentheus) between 'the superior ones', the unbelievers, and those who think and feel as other men:

> ... the god hates those to whom these things are not important, namely, to live one's life, day and friendly night, in happiness, and to keep a wise mind and heart away from the too clever ones (*perissôn para phôtôn*). What the common majority of men (*to plêthos ... to phauloteron*) thinks and practises (*enomise chrêtai te*), that *I* would accept. (*Bacch.* 424-32)

Once again, we should note that 'what every men thinks and practises', i.e. the *nomoi* (as this is called elsewhere in the play, e.g. at 331, 484, 891, 895; note also *enomise*, 424, in the present passage), has now become, in the Chorus' formulations, the touchstone of the new religion.

It is interesting to note that in the following episode, in the first of what might be called 'the cat and mouse exchanges' between the bullying King and his divine captive, a similar contrast is made between the *nomoi* (in a *good* sense) of the *barbaroi* (484), who dance the sacred dances, and those of the sophisticated Greeks (like Pentheus) who won't.

The activities and attitudes of the Bacchants have been consistently presented as their *nomoi* and, thanks to the words of Teiresias and the songs of the Chorus, those *nomoi* have been shown to have their roots in ancestral tradition and in timeless chthonic cults. One further (dare one call it 'philosophic'?) step remains to be taken and once again it is the wild and, after their fashion, 'wise' Chorus of maenads who take it.

The third stasimon (862ff.) marks the choral turning point in the play. It comes at the crucial moment in the dramatic action, the moment after Pentheus has re-entered the palace under the spell of the god, and before he comes out, his wits driven from him and his limbs clothed in the victim's ritual garb.

The ode begins with the lovely 'escaping fawn' image, in which the Bacchant, 'setting her white foot down in the all-night dances and tossing her head in the dewy air', is likened to a fawn escaping the nets of the hunters (as the Theban women have escaped Pentheus) and 'racing along the plain by the river, delighting in the solitude and in the thickets of the shadowy woods' (873-6).

The antistrophe turns from escape to vengeance but first comes the brief refrain:

> What price cleverness? (*ti to sophon;*) Or rather, what is a nobler prize from the gods than to hold a victorious hand over one's enemies? ... (*Bacch.* 876ff.)

But the following stanza (882ff.) invoking the avenging power of the divine, like so many passionate utterances of this maenad Chorus, slips into almost philosophic musings before it is completed:

> [The god] chastises those who honour insensitive arrogance (*agnômosunê*) and, in their madness, fail to encourage pursuits dear to the gods ... For it is not right, it is not permitted (*ou chrê*) to seek knowledge and practice beyond the traditional customs (*kreissôn ... tôn nomôn*). For it is not hard to understand that whatever is divine must prevail and that whatever has been the custom for a long period of time (*to t' en chronôi makrôi*

> *nomimon*, 895) is eternal, and grounded in nature (*aei phusêi te pephukos*, 896). (*Bacch.* 884-96, in part)

(I follow Dodds' construing of the last sentence, above, and his comments on it in his note *ad loc.*)

This whole passage once again contrasts the arrogance of the 'unbeliever' such as Pentheus with the saner intelligence of the common man, the true Dionysian in the opinion of the Bacchants. Again, the beliefs and practices of the latter are identified with the traditional *nomoi* (e.g. at 895-6, though the idea is prepared for at 891-2). Thus the last sentence of the passage seems to reflect both Sophistic influence and the poet's own originality, or, at least, perceptiveness, as Dodds' observations here well indicate:

> ... the Chorus anticipate in principle Plato's solution of the *nomos-phusis* antinomy, viz. that when the two terms are properly understood *nomos* is seen to be founded upon *phusis* (*Laws* 890D ...). Similarly the late-fifth-century writer known as Anonymus Iamblichi argues *ton te nomon kai to dikaion embasileuein tois anthrôpois kai oudamêi metastênai an auta: phusêi gar ischura endedesthai tauta* [that *nomos* ('law', or 'custom'?) and justice rule over men and would never be likely to be separated: for they have been firmly bound together by nature].[18]
>
> (Diels, *Vors.* ii, p. 402.28ff.).

Whether the author known as Anonymus Iamblichi belonged to the late fifth century or to the early early fourth century, he was no doubt influenced by Sophistic thought. It is perhaps impossible to decide between Euripides and this anonymous author as to which was the first to provide the earliest extant statement of the close relation between *nomos* and *phusis* when, as Dodds puts it, 'the two terms are properly understood', but which had for so long been treated as antithetical concepts. Nor, indeed, does this matter greatly since both authors were in all probability developing, or possibly repeating, a view enunciated by one or another of their Sophistic contemporaries or near-contemporaries.

While the *Bacchae* reflects Sophistic subtlety in its distinctions between, and blendings of, related ideas, it also seems to imply certain criticisms (whether shared by the poet, we cannot say) of Sophistic attitudes toward traditional beliefs and even toward popular culture. These occur in the Chorus' reactions to Pentheus' arrogant disbelief and persecution, if we give their comments on 'too clever men' and the like a contemporary application. We may perhaps quote a few of these again, to indicate their relevance in a wider context.

to sophon ou sophia, 'Cleverness is not wisdom', is a refrain of the Chorus. 'Nor is it wisdom', they continue, 'to think more than mortal thoughts' (395-6). Again, the Chorus suggests that 'the god hates the man ... who does not keep a wise mind and heart away from the too clever ones (*perissôn para phôtôn*, 429) ... What the common man thinks and makes use of, that *I* would accept' (424-32, in part). These are not the thoughts of a Sophist; far from it (see, for example, Protagoras' agnostic remarks at D-K 80 B4). And it is Pentheus' arrogant cleverness which leads the Chorus and also Teiresias (266ff., cf. 200-3) and even Cadmus (at 232) to indict Pentheus, and it is this characteristic which spells his ruin in the play.

It is ironic that Teiresias uses the word *katabalei* at 202, in his criticism of the too clever ones who might seek to overthrow the ancestral traditions on the gods. As several scholars have observed, this word appears as the title of Protagoras' 'Destructive Essays' (*Kataballontes* sc. *Logoi* (D-K 80 B1), which may have contained his comments on the gods.[19]

Teiresias' own position, is, in the context of the present discussion, a little difficult to pin down. On the one hand he does, as we have seen, criticize Pentheus' arrogant cleverness and disbelief in Dionysus; on the other hand, we have also noted that his own comments on Demeter and Dionysus at 274ff. seem to have something in common with Prodicus' views as cited at D-K 84 B5.[20] We should consider also the interesting views of Deichgräber, who regards not only Teiresias and Cadmus but even Dionysus himself as 'Sophistic' and who suggests that the Chorus are the only true Dionysians in the play![21] It is true, of course, that Teiresias himself is called *sophos* three times by Cadmus (at 179 twice, and once at 186, as has been noted already); clearly it is a term which he must accept. (It is interesting that the term *sophos* also keeps occurring in 'the cat and mouse scenes' between Dionysus and Pentheus, e.g. at 480, 655, 656, 824.) But Teiresias insists (see again 200ff.) that for mortals true wisdom cannot concern itself with divine matters, with matters beyond mortal ken and that 'cleverness' will never overthrow ancestral traditions. This is the fault, among others, of Pentheus ... but it is also the fault, in terms of the implications of this play, of Sophistic rationalism. Thus we should not, I think, simply dismiss the Teiresias of this play (as Deichgräber seems to do) as a Sophist.

This same fruitful paradox, if one may so describe it, is found in the Chorus. The Chorus represents the *new* god, and yet, since choral odes are dramatically timeless, it can also associate Dionysian mystery with age-old mythical traditions. Moreover, the Chorus, like Teiresias, expresses the contrast between wisdom and cleverness (395f.) – a contrast which reflects the conflict between the rhetorical cleverness of much of the Sophistic movement and the true wisdom which occasionally gleams behind a few of its preserved utterances.

VII

Conclusion

I introduced this book with an apology for its limitations, pointing out that it would be concerned not with Euripides as a philosophical or political thinker but rather with some of his dramatic and original treatments of various philosophical teachings and ideas (especially of the Sophists) of his time. A brief review, in this Conclusion, should, however, serve to indicate Euripides' lively engagement and, in some cases, deep concern with the various issues which he dramatized in such a variety of ways. We should not, of course, expect detailed analysis of these issues, for this is tragedy, not philosophy. Sometimes, to be sure, the poet did suggest his own attitudes to them, but for him to have done so too explicitly might well have spoiled the subtle treatments which I have attempted to describe.

I began with questions raised in *Hippolytus* about a particularly Sophistic (and Socratic) concern: whether virtue comes by nature (*phusis*) or whether it is teachable – and if the latter, how (if at all) one can be sure of attaining virtue, even if one knows what is right? Here we witnessed Hippolytus' own certainty that *aidôs* and *sôphrosunê* (which for him comprised the whole of virtue) came by nature only and that he, Hippolytus, was indeed *sôphrôn*. Soon afterwards, we have seen Phaedra, in contrast to the supremely self-confident Hippolytus, agonizing over the question to reach the bitter conclusion that various distractions, including the distractions of pleasure, may (*pace* Socrates) prevent one from doing the good one knows. Finally, Theseus, wrongly suspecting the chaste Hippolytus, throws up his hands in despair that no one knows how to teach virtue to those who have it not. None of these very different characters achieve virtue and for each the action of the play brings catastrophe.

In *Alcestis* (as we have seen in Chapter III), Euripides treats the Sophistic topic 'the relativity of virtue' in connection particularly with the ambiguous (and typically Greek) virtue of *charis*, 'favour owed for favour received'. Admetus, attempting to fulfil the virtue of *xenia* ('hospitality') to his friend Heracles, betrays the obligations of *charis*, which he owes to his deceased wife, who has done him the great favour of dying in his place. Admetus now discovers that his own life (saved, at Alcestis' expense, owing to Apollo's 'return of favour' to Admetus) is no longer worth living without Alcestis. However, the dramatist saves the action from being tragic by enclosing it within a folk-tale frame. Heracles returns Admetus' favour by miraculously restoring Alcestis, and so ensures a happy ending to this ironic *jeu d'esprit*.

In my 'intermezzo' in Chapter IV, between the chapters dealing with various themes drawn from the philosophical teachings of the Sophists, I have noted two rather different reflections of Sophistic rhetoric and its effects in *Troades* and in *Hecuba*, respectively. In the *agôn* between Helen and Hecuba, in *Troades*, Euripides seems to be indulging his own rhetorical, even eristic, skills with the enjoyment of the virtuoso outdoing even the Sophists by his dramatic treatment of a well-known rhetorical theme. In *Hecuba*, on the other hand, the poet, in more sombre mode, seems to suggest a clear relation between rhetorical power and blinkered moral vision in the case of Odysseus and between rhetorical effectiveness and moral decline in the case of Hecuba herself. *Helen* (discussed in Chapter V) is the only play we have considered in which Euripides (at least in my opinion) has provided a clearly satirical treatment of Sophistic themes. In any case, the comic possibilities of presenting Sophistic views of the equal 'reality' of all our sense perceptions in the context of the Stesichorean 'wraith version' of the Helen myth, seem to have proved irresistible. Nevertheless, Euripides also succeeded in employing even this light-hearted treatment in the service of a serious theme: the delusions causing not only the Trojan War but also all other wars, including that war, so disastrous for Athens, now drawing to a close.

In our review in Chapter VI of the concept of *nomos* and related ideas (especially *phusis*) in Sophistic thought, we found several ideas which reappear, in a variety of contexts, in Euripidean drama, expecially in plays dealing with social and political situations, such as *Supplices* and *Heraclidae.*

In *Supplices*, we have noted Theseus' account, in his first response to the Argive suppliant Adrastus, of the evolution of the well-ordered society (a particularly Sophistic style of demonstration), which provides the basis for his subsequent defence of the suppliants. *Nomos* in *Supplices* is emphasized specifically in connection with the burial of the dead, which is now seen, perhaps for the first time, as a part of panhellenic law, and here we remember the essential role of *nomos* in Protagoras' account, in his myth of Prometheus, of the origin of society.

In *Heraclidae*, issues relating to law and justice arise again in connection with a supplication theme, as Iolaus urges the claims of *aidôs* and *dikê* (two virtues also prominent in Protagoras' civilization myth) in his plea to Athens for defence of the Heraclidae. The Argive Herald, on the other hand, urges the advantage (*kerdos*) to be gained by siding with the stronger against the weaker power. Nowhere else in Euripides is the struggle between *nomos* and *phusis*, seen here as the rule of civilized values against the rule of the strong, more vividly expressed.

Of the several paradoxes which we found in Euripides' *Bacchae*, perhaps the most fundamental one concerns *nomos* and *phusis*, the most characteristic of Sophistic binary concepts. On the one hand, we have Pentheus, the epitome of law and order, and on the other, the wild and naturalistic cult of Dionysus, which Pentheus fears would destroy that order. Yet the claim of the Bacchants of the Dionysian Chorus is that their way of life is true to their *nomoi*, the age-old traditions (*patrioi paradochai*), as Teiresias calls them, and Pentheus is finally destroyed through his own corrupt and voyeuristic vision of the Bacchants. Related to this paradox is the treatment of age and youth, and of true wisdom contrasted with the (Sophistic?) cleverness of Pentheus. The resolution of the central paradox, as I have called it, is perhaps indicated in the last song of the Chorus before it turns to vengeance, namely, that the age-old customs (*nomoi*) which it champions are actually based on human nature (*phusis*). This (as has been noted) reflects at least a hint of a similar reconciliation of the ancient antinomy in at least one extant Sophistic passage.

One senses that the paradoxical presentation, in this masterpiece of the poet's old age, of traditional ways and new ideas, may reflect something of the conflicts, emotional and intellectual, within Euripides himself.

Conspectus of Sophists

This conspectus provides brief indications of the main teachings and interests attributed to the Sophists mentioned in this book. Precise biographical information for these Sophists is lacking, though they are known to have flourished in the second half of the fifth century BC, and thus to have been contemporaries (some older, some younger) of Euripides. Works attributed to them have all perished except for fragments and doxographical reports of their teachings, as described in Chapter I. (See also the works of Kathleen Freeman and the recent work of M. Gagarin and P. Woodruff among others listed in the Bibliography.)

I have listed the relatively few Sophists concerned in order of their relevance to this study.

Protagoras of Abdera is, perhaps, the first and best known of the Sophists. He visited Athens at least twice before the Peloponnesian War, and possibly later, where he lectured and claimed to have been the first to teach 'political virtue'. He wrote a book variously called *Truth*, *Refutations* and *On Being*, and another book, *On the Gods*. He is particularly celebrated for the (variously interpreted) dictum, 'Man is the measure of all things', and for his claims that there are two contradictory arguments on everything and that he could make the weaker argument appear the stronger.

Gorgias of Leontini, though best known as one of the early teachers of rhetoric, and as the author of handbooks on rhetoric, also lectured and wrote on philosophical topics, as his essay *On Being* or *On Nature* indicates. Two of his model orations, his *Defence of Palamedes* and *Encomium of Helen*, have survived in whole or in part. He appears, both from the latter work and from Socrates' comments in Plato's dialogues, to have been quite candid in his emphasis on the function of rhetoric as *persuasion*, even, if necessary, at the expense of truth.

Antiphon is one of the most interesting and also most puzzling of the Sophists. Unlike many Sophists, he seems to have been an Athenian and to have lived most of his life in Athens. He wrote a major philosophical work, *Truth*, as well as several rhetorical essays, unless, as some scholars think, 'Antiphon the Sophist' and 'Antiphon the Orator' were two separate individuals.

To judge from some fragments of his philosophical work, Antiphon presented paradoxical arguments on justice and on the dictates of law contrasted with those of nature, and held sophisticated views on the self-sufficiency of the gods. His observations on 'nature' (*phusis*) led him to deprecate the contrast supported by many Athenians between Greeks and 'barbarians'.

Prodicus of Ceos was a well-known and (according to the Platonic Socrates) quite an expensive teacher of rhetoric who visited and taught at Athens. (Socrates and Euripides were both alleged to have attended some of his lectures.) Prodicus also wrote books on the nature of things, on cosmology and on the nature of the gods; belief in the gods, and the nature of the gods of myth he explained as the attribution of divinity to whatever was useful to human beings.

Prodicus was particularly noted for his concern for precise definitions (especially of various qualities, such as 'courage' and 'daring'), for the correct naming of things and for the distinctions between things which were, in his view, wrongly treated as synonymous. The Platonic Socrates and Aristotle tended to be critical of some of these as over-refinements; however, this concern of Prodicus may have been a useful contribution to semantics.

Critias came of a wealthy Athenian family, known for its pro-Spartan sympathies. He was an extreme oligarch and a leader of the oligarchical coup of 'the Thirty' in 404. Critias perished in the overthrow of the Thirty in the following year.

Critias was not himself a Sophist, though he apparently associated with Sophists and shared the interests and views of some of them. He was a polished orator and also the author of poems (including one on *Constitutions*) and plays. In his satyr-play, *Sisyphus* (which some attribute to Euripides), the view is expressed that the gods were invented to induce men to obey the laws.

Thrasymachus of Chalcedon travelled to many places, including Athens. He was known mainly as a teacher of rhetoric but is best known to posterity for his aggressive insistence in Book I of Plato's *Republic* that justice is the advantage of the stronger. Plato's picture of Thrasymachus here may not, however, accurately represent his views on justice; there has even been some disagreement about the identity of the Platonic Thrasymachus.

Bibliography

This bibliography is restricted to works referred to in the book and to a few additional items found useful in its preparation. (Asterisks mark items which may be particularly useful for the general reader.)

Editions and translations

Barrett, W.S., ed., *Euripides, Hippolytus*. Oxford, 1964

Bond, G., ed., *Euripides, Heracles*. Oxford, 1981

*Collard, C., ed. and trans., *Euripides, Heracles*. Warminster, 1991

——— ed., *Euripides, Supplices*, vol. 2. Groningen, 1975

*Conacher, D.J., ed. and trans., *Euripides, Alcestis*. Warmister, 1961

Dale, A.M., ed., *Euripides, Alcestis*. Oxford, 1954

——— ed., *Euripides, Helen*. Oxford, 1967

Diels, H., ed., *Die Fragmente der Vorsokratiker*, herausgegeben von Walther Kranz, 6th ed. Berlin, 1954

Diggle, J., ed., *Euripidis Fabulae*, vols. 1 and 2. Oxford, 1981, 1984

Dodds, E.R., ed., *Euripides, Bacchae*, 2nd ed. Oxford, 1959

*Gagarin, M. & Woodruff, P., eds., *Early Greek Political Thought from Homer to the Sophists*. Cambridge, 1995

Kranz, W., ed., *see* Diels

*Morrison, J.S. and Sprague, R., eds., *The Older Sophists*. Columbia, 1972

Murray, G., ed., *Euripidis Fabulae*, 3 vols, 3rd ed. Oxford, 1913

Reesor, M., trans., *Anonymus Iamblichi*, see Morrison and Sprague

Robinson, T.M., ed., *Contrasting Arguments: An Edition of the Dissoi Logoi*. New York, 1979

Sprague, R. *see* Morrison

*Way, A.S., *Euripides with an English translation*, vol 1. London and New York, 1920

*Woodruff, P., *see* Gagarin

Books

*Burian, P., ed., *Directions in Euripidean Criticism*. Durham, 1985

Burnett, A., *Catastrophe Survived*. Oxford, 1971.

*Buxton, R., *Persuasion in Greek Tragedy*. Cambridge, 1982

Classen, C.J., ed., *Sophistik, Wege der Forschung* 187. Darmstadt, 1976

Conacher, D.J., *Aeschylus, Prometheus Bound, a literary commentary*. Toronto, 1980

*——— *Euripidean Drama, Myth, Theme and Structure*. Toronto and London, 1967

Croally, N., *Euripidean Polemic, The Trojan Women and the Function of Greek Tragedy*. Cambridge, 1994

Decharme, P., *Euripides and the Spirit of his Dramas*, trans., James Loeb. New York, 1906

*Dodds, E.R., *The Ancient Concept of Progress*. Oxford, 1973

——— *The Greeks and the Irrational*. Berkeley and Los Angeles, 1959

*Easterling, P. and Muir, J., eds., *Greek Religion and Society*. Cambridge, 1985

——— ed., *The Cambridge History of Classical Literature*, vol. I, parts 1 and 2. Cambridge, 1989

Freeman, K., *Ancilla to the Pre-Socratic Philosophers*. Oxford, 1948

——— *see also* Untersteiner

Goldhill, S., *Reading Greek Tragedy*. Cambridge, 1986

Gregory, J., *Euripides and the Instruction of the Athenians*. Ann Arbor, 1981

*Guthrie, W.K.C., *The Sophists*. Cambridge, 1971 (= Part I of vol. 3 of *A History of Greek Philosophy*. Cambridge, 1969)

Hall, E., *Inventing the Barbarian*. Oxford, 1989

Heinimann, F., *Nomos und Physis*. Basel, 1965

*Kerferd, G.B., *The Sophists*. Cambridge, 1981

Lloyd, M., *The Agon in Euripides*. Oxford, 1992

Lupher, D., *Persuasion and Politics in Euripides*. Stanford University dissertation, 1979

*Michelini, A., *Euripides and the Tragic Tradition*. Madison, 1987

Mossman, J., *Wild Justice*. Oxford, 1995

*Muir, J. *see* Easterling

Nestle, W., *Euripides der Dichter der griechischen Aufklärung*. Stuttgart, 1901

Nussbaum, M., *The Fragility of Goodness*. Cambridge, 1986

Ostwald, M., *Nomos and the Beginnings of the Athenian Democracy*. Oxford, 1969

Scodel, R., *The Trojan Trilogy*. Gottingen, 1980

Snell, B., *Scenes from Greek Tragedy*. Berkeley and Los Angeles, 1964

Untersteiner, M., *The Sophists*, trans. K. Freeman. Oxford, 1954

Vlastos, G., *Socrates, Ironist and Moral Philosopher*. Cambridge, 1991
Winnington-Ingram, R.P., *Euripides and Dionysus*. Cambridge, 1948

Articles

Burian, P., '*Logos* and *Pathos*: The Politics of *The Suppliant Women*', *Directions in Euripidean Criticism*, 129-55, ed. Peter Burian. Durham, 1985
Chalk, H., '*Aretê* and *Bia* in the *Heracles*', *JHS* 82 (1962), 7-18
Classen, C., 'The Study of Language', *Sophistik*, 215-47, ed. C. Classen. Darmstadt, 1976
Claus, D., 'Phaedra and the Socratic Paradox', *Yale Classical Studies* 22 (1972), 223-38
Collard, C., 'Formal Debates in Euripidean Drama', *G&R* 22 (1975), 58-71
Conacher, D.J., 'Rhetoric and Relevance in Euripidean Drama', *AJP* (1981), 3-25
——— 'Questions of Probability and Relevance in Euripidean Drama', *Maia* 24 (1972), 199-207
Deichgräber, K., 'Die Kadmos-Teiresias Szene in Euripides' *Bakchen*', *Hermes* 70 (1935), 322-49
Dodds, E.R., 'The *Aidôs* of Phaedra and the Meaning of the *Hippolytus*', *CR* (1925), 102-4
Griffith, J., 'Some Thoughts on *Helena*', *JHS* 73 (1953), 36-41
Kerferd, G., 'The Doctrine of Thrasymachus in Plato's *Republic*', *Durham University Journal* (1947), 19-27, reprinted in *Sophistik*, 545-63, ed. C. Classen. Darmstadt, 1976
Kirkwood, G., 'Hecuba and *Nomos*', *TAPA* 78 (1947), 61-8
Maguire, J., 'Thrasymachus or Plato?', *Phronesis* 16 (1971), 142-63, reprinted in *Sophistik*, 564-90, ed. C. Classen. Darmstadt, 1976
Muir, J., 'Religion and the New Education', *Religion and Society*, 204-15, ed. P. Easterling and J. Muir. Cambridge, 1985
Pippin, A., 'Euripides' *Helen*: A Comedy of Ideas', *CP* 55 (1960), 151-63
Reckford, K., 'Concepts of Demoralization in *Hecuba*', *Directions in Euripidean Criticism*, 122-8, ed. P. Burian. Durham, 1985
Segal, C., 'Gorgias and the Psychology of the *Logos*', *HSCP* 66 (1962), 99-155
Sinclair, T., 'Socrates and his Opponents', *Sophistik*, 67-196, ed. C. Classen. Darmstadt, 1976
Solmsen, F., '*Onoma* and *Pragma* in Euripides' *Helen*', *CR* (1934) 119-21
Vernant, J.-P., 'Greek Tragedy: Problems of Interpretation', in *The Structuralist Controversy*, 273-88, ed. Richard Macksey and Eugenio Donato. Baltimore and London, 1972

Notes

I. Introduction

1. Of the many studies of the Sophists, several of which will be referred to below, see particularly M. Untersteiner, *The Sophists*, translated by Kathleen Freeman (Oxford, 1954); W.K.C. Guthrie, *The Sophists* (Cambridge, 1971) = vol. III, part 1 of his *A History of Greek Philosophy* (Cambridge, 1969); C.J. Classen, ed., *Sophistik, Wege der Forschung* 187 (Darmstadt, 1976) and bibliography there given; G.B. Kerferd, *The Sophists* (Cambridge, 1981).

2. Hermann Diels, *Die Fragmente der Vorsokratiker*, herausgegeben von Walther Kranz (6th ed.; Berlin, 1954), pp. 252-405.

3. Concerning the degree to which it is possible to distinguish truly Socratic ideas in the dialogues of Plato, see particularly Gregory Vlastos, *Socrates, Ironist and Moral Philosopher* (Cambridge, 1991), pp. 45ff. Vlastos regards the philosophy attributed to Socrates in Plato's earlier dialogues (which include any referred to in the present study) as '*that of the historical Socrates* recreated by Plato in invented conversations which explore its content and exhibit its method' (p. 49).

4. Wilhelm Nestle, *Euripides, der Dichter der griechischen Aufklärung* (Stuttgart, 1901); Paul Decharme, *Euripides and the Spirit of his Dramas*, translated by James Loeb (New York, 1906).

5. See Nestle (1901), pp. 4-6 and pp. 46-9.

6. Nestle, p. 47.

7. See Decharme (1906), pp. 20-42.

8. Decharme, pp. 34-42.

9. Decharme, pp. 41-2.

10. Decharme, p. 42.

11. Mario Untersteiner, *The Sophists*, translated by Kathleen Freeman (Oxford, 1954).

12. See Untersteiner, p. 4 and n. 3.

13. N.T. Croally, *Euripidean Polemic, The Trojan Women and the Function of Tragedy* (Cambridge, 1994), esp. pp. 10, 19-20, 166, 221ff.; Simon

Goldhill, *Reading Greek Tragedy* (Cambridge, 1986); J.P. Vernant, 'Greek Tragedy: Problems of Interpretation' in *The Structuralist Controversy*, ed. Richard Macksey and Eugenio Donato, (Baltimore and London, 1972).

14. Peter Burian, ed., *Directions in Euripidean Criticism* (Durham, 1955), including Burian's own article, '*Logos* and *Pathos*: The Politics of the *Suppliant Women*', pp. 129-55; R.G.A. Buxton, *Persuasion in Greek Tragedy* (Cambridge, 1982), ch. 1 *passim*, and ch. 5, pp. 187ff.; C.J. Classen ed., *Sophistik*, Darmstadt (1976), including Classen's own article, 'The Study of Language', pp. 215-47; Christopher Collard, 'Formal Debates in Euripidean Drama', *G&R* (1975), pp. 58-71; Justina Gregory, *Euripides and the Instruction of the Athenians* (Ann Arbor, 1991), 'Introduction' (this study tends, perhaps, to over-emphasize the didactic element in Euripides, particularly on political matters); Michael Lloyd, *The Agon in Euripides* (Oxford, 1992), pp. 28-35; and Ann M. Michelini, *Euripides and the Tragic Tradition* (Madison, 1987), pp. 52ff., 71, 120, 126-7, 273-89 (at pp. 126-7, Michelini considers Euripides as 'the voice of the Sophists', but at pp. 40-1 she considers occasional 'anti-Sophist' views of the poet as well).

15. Explanations of Euripides' intention in this passage of the *Heracles* will, of course, vary with our interpretation of the play as a whole and with our view of the relation of the passage to its context. For the interpretation implied in the explanation suggested above, see my *Euripidean Drama*, ch. 4, especially pp. 88-90. For very different views of this passage, see H.O.O. Chalk, '*Arete* and *Bia* in the *Herakles*', *JHS* 82 (1962), pp. 7-18 and, especially, Godfrey Bond in his note to ll. 1341-6, in his edition of *Euripides, Heracles* (Oxford, 1981), and references there given. Bond, for example, explains this passage as a direct and detailed answer to the argument of Theseus (1314-21) – which, of course, it is. This does not, however, remove the fact that it is also glaringly inconsistent with the views of the gods, particularly of Hera, which Heracles expresses before and after this passage, and, indeed, with the plot and situation of the whole play. This inconsistency would have struck even an audience of Euripides' day and so must surely have been intentional. It is hardly sufficient to dismiss such a difficulty with a reference to 'the rhetoric of the situation' (A.M. Dale's phrase, in the Introduction to her edition of Euripides' *Alcestis* [Oxford, 1954], pp. xxivff.), and with a sneer at Verrall. One does not have to be a Verrall to find *HF* 1341ff. exceptional, even for Euripides.

16. See Dodds' interesting note on *Bacchae* 274-85, including his discussion whether the view which Prodicus described was itself a literal belief or a rationalization of a literal belief.

II. The Nature and Teachability of Virtue

1. We are not here concerned with Socrates' appeal, in the course of this demonstration, and its apparent implications, to a hedonistic calculus of pleasure relevant to the dialectical level of the Platonic discussion at this point.

2. This sudden shift by the Queen from the near hysteria of her earlier utterances to the sustained intellectual reasoning of the present passage need not concern us here. Such switching from one to another aspect of a character's *persona* is a not unusual feature of Euripidean drama; see my discussion of such passages in 'Rhetoric and Relevance in Euripidean Drama', *AJP* (1981), pp. 3-25.

3. I follow Barrett (W.S. Barrett, *Euripides, Hippolytus* [Oxford, 1964], in his note *ad loc.*) in not taking *aidôs* as one of 'the pleasures', though not, as we shall see, in his interpretation of *aidôs.*

4. There has been protracted debate among Classicists on these points. Bruno Snell, in his *Scenes from Greek Tragedy* (Berkeley and Los Angeles, 1964), pp. 48-69, is the strongest exponent of the 'anti-Socratic' intent of the passage. Barrett, at the end of his note to *Hipp.* 377-81, argues strenuously against Snell's view as previously expressed in *Philologus* 97 (1948), pp. 125ff. E.R. Dodds, *The Greeks and the Irrational* (Berkeley and Los Angeles, 1959), supports a less extreme version of Snell's view, while David Claus, 'Phaedra and the Socratic Paradox', *Yale Classical Studies* 22 (1972), pp. 223-38, rejects Snell's argument on the grounds that Phaedra, at 426-7, actually *vindicates* the efforts of her own *gnômê.* For more recent discussion of the issue, see Ann Michelini, *Euripides and the Tragic Tradition* (Madison, Wisconsin 1987), p. 304, cf. p. 297, who sees the passage as 'a tribute to Socratic influence [rather than as] a "polemic" against the philosopher'.

5. See E.R. Dodds, 'The *AIDÔS* of Phaedra and the Meaning of the *Hippolytus*', *CR* 39 (1925), 102-4, to whom I am indebted for this explanation of 'the bad *aidôs*'; I do not, however, agree with Dodds' further attempt to show that this act of *aidôs* on Phaedra's part is also to be understood as one of the *pleasures* which distract one from doing the good one knows.

6. Cf., again, Dodds, *ibid.*, p. 103.

7. See above, Chapter II, p. 31, where the fragment of Antiphon is quoted in full.

8. See Barrett's note to *Hipp.* 921.

III. The Relativity of Virtue

1. Kerferd, *The Sophistic Movement*, ch. 9: his discussion of Sophistic relativism suggests the interconnectedness of this subject in the fields of ethics, epistemology and even rhetoric.

2. See D-K II, p. 405, note to 90.1. For a translation of the *Dissoi Logoi*, see T.M. Robinson, *Contrasting Arguments: An Edition of the Dissoi Logoi* (New York, 1979).

3. See D-K 87 B44, A; for this and the following translation from Antiphon (87) B44, A and B, see J.S. Morrison in Rosamund Sprague, *The Older Sophists* (Columbia, S.C., 1972), pp. 219ff.

4. See above, Chapter II, pp. 28-40, especially pp. 28-31.

5. I shall be considering this version in more detail, in another context, in Chapter V below.

IV. The Power and Abuses of Rhetoric

1. On various aspects of *agônes* (debates) in Euripides, and on rhetorical and other influences on them, see, among other studies, C. Collard, 'Formal Debates in Euripidean Drama,' *G&R* 22 (1975), pp. 58-71; Michael Lloyd, *The Agon in Euripides* (Oxford, 1992), esp. ch. 2 and references there given; N.T. Croally, *Euripidean Polemic, The Trojan Women and the Function of Tragedy* (Cambridge, 1994), esp. ch. 3. Cf. also my article, 'Rhetoric and Relevance in Euripidean Drama', *AJP* 102 (1981), pp. 3-25.

2. On these sudden and improbable shifts of mood between a character's lyrical and dramatic utterances, see my article, 'Questions of Probability and Relevance in Euripidean Drama', *Maia* 24 (1972), pp. 199-207.

3. Croally (1994), pp. 221-2. He observes further (p. 125; cf. p. 255) that in this passage Euripides might also be criticizing Athenian imperial policy, especially war policy. Cf. J.-P. Vernant, 'Greek Tragedy: Problems of Interpretation', in E. Donato and R. Macksey, eds., *The Structuralist Controversy* (Baltimore, 1970), to which Croally also refers.

4. Cf. Lloyd (1992), pp. 22ff.

5. Lloyd (1992), pp. 100ff. Cf. Segal (1962), pp. 99-155.

6. Ruth Scodel, *The Trojan Trilogy* (Gottingen, 1980), pp. 96ff.

7. See below, n. 12.

8. Scodel (1980), p. 99.

9. Croally (1994); the following quotations are from pp. 144-5.

10. In addition to Scodel and Croally, see also Guthrie (1971), p. 92, n. 2, and Goldhill (1986), pp. 236-8.

11. The similarity in the Gorgian and Euripidean references to 'seeing' (*opsis*, *Enc*. 15.5, and *idôn*, *Tro*. 988, respectively), in connection with the physical aspect of *erôs*, has also been noted by Scodel (1980), pp. 98-9.

12. Croally (1994), p. 156.

13. See, for example, Michelini (1987), ch. 6, esp. sections III and VI; R.G.A. Buxton, *Persuasion in Greek Tragedy* (Cambridge, 1982), pp. 170-88; Lloyd (1992), ch. 2, *passim*. Cf. also Conacher (1967), ch. 8, and (1981), pp. 3-25.

14. See above, Chapter III.

15. Cf. also comments by Michelini (1987), pp. 144-5 and Buxton (1982), p. 172.

16. Buxton (1982), p. 175.

17. On this passage on *nomos*, see below, Chapter VI, p. 89.

18. C. Collard, ed., *Euripides, Supplices* (Warminster 1991), in his note *ad loc*. See also his references to other occurrences of this myth.

19. On the relation between rhetoric and drama in this and other Euripidean plays, see also Conacher (1981), pp. 3-25; Buxton (1982), pp. 170 and 182-6; Michelini (1987), p. 142; Mossman, *Wild Justice* (Oxford, 1995), ch. 4. We should note also Buxton's wise reminder that the pejorative presentation of rhetoric in *Hecuba* does not indicate the poet's general view of the art: he cites *Supplices* 349ff. and other passages in this play as more positive presentations of rhetoric.

20. See Kenneth J. Reckford, 'Concepts of Demoralization in *Hecuba*', in *Directions in Euripidean Criticism*, ed. Peter Burian, pp. 122-8, and Martha Nussbaum, *The Fragility of Goodness* (Cambridge 1986), pp. 399-405. But cf. also Gordon M. Kirkwood, '*Hecuba* and *nomos*', *TAPA* 78 (1947), pp. 61-8, who finds the turning point of the play to be when Hecuba turns from *nomos* to *peithô* ('persuasion').

21. See Mossman (1995), ch. 6, esp. pp. 16ff., 174ff., 177ff. and her excellent account of various views of other biographical studies of the play. Cf. also her ch. 4, esp. pp. 121-2.

22. See Collard in his Introduction to *Supplices* (1991), p. 23.

23. Cf. Guthrie (1971), pp. 122ff. and nn. 2 and 4 to p. 153. Cf. also Goldhill (1986), p. 227.

24. See Croally (1994), pp. 111ff.

25. Edith Hall, *Inventing the Barbarian: Greek Self-Definition through Tragedy* (Oxford, 1989), pp. 160-1. Hall also refers to M.L. Apte, *Humor and Laughter: an Anthropological Approach* (Ithaca and London, 1985) in this connection. For the second point from Hall discussed above, see *Inventing the Barbarians*, ch. VI, especially pp. 211ff.

V. Reality and Sense Perception

1. See, for example, Kerferd (1981), pp. 86-7; Guthrie (1971) p. 183ff. and references there given. Cf. also Untersteiner (1954), pp. 41ff., who has more confidence than some scholars have in Sextus' credibility in this matter.

2. The doctrine of the Sophists (or at least of a few of the Sophists) on 'names' and on definitions has already been considered in Chapter II above, in connection with the treatment of the ambiguity attaching to certain 'virtues'. In what follows, we shall be concerned with this doctrine in quite a different context: the use of names in connection with the identification of the objective reality of persons and things. It seems best, for the convenience of the reader, to repeat the Sophistic references given in the former passage, along with a few additional references relevant to the present context.

3. Kerferd's translation (1981, p. 73) in his discussion, in ch. 7, of Prodicus' doctrine on this matter.

4. See also the excellent discussion of this play by Ann N. Pippin in 'Euripides' *Helen*: A Comedy of Ideas', *CP* 55 (1960), pp. 151-63, to which my own studies of the *Helen*, both here and earlier, are indebted. Cf. also her later treatment of *Helen* in *Catastrophe Survived* (Oxford, 1971), ch. 4. See also Conacher (1967), ch. 16.

5. Stesichorus composed one or possibly two 'palinodes' on Helen in which he replaced the unflattering presentation of her which he had given in his (also lost) earlier ode on Helen. (Both legendary and 'political' explanations have been given for Stesichorus' recantation.) The precise details of the palinode(s) remain controversial. It seems certain that Stesichorus invented the wraith of Helen and its substitution for the real Helen at Troy, and probably the sojourn of the real Helen in Egypt under the protection there of King Proteus, though how she might have reached Egypt in Stesichorus' version remains a mystery. For fuller summaries of this matter (including in particular the various sources involved), see Conacher (1967), pp. 286-9, and, more recently and more authoritively, *The Cambridge History of Classical Literature*, vol. I, part I, ed. P.E. Easterling and B.M.W. Knox (1989), ch. 5, 'Archaic and Choral Lyric' (by Charles Segal), pp. 150-1.

6. I do not accept Reiske's rejection of *kai nous horâi*, an expression which Dale also rejects as improbable in the context. The sentence does seem to me to be relevant, at least to the dramatist's treatment of Sophistic views of sense perception as we have been discussing it in these passages (and certainly more relevant to this than to the line of Epicharmus [see Dale's note *ad loc.*] to which some critics think it alludes). Since sense perceptions, and particularly those of sight, are regarded by the Sophists as the only source of reality, it is not inappropriate that Teucer, talking for a moment like a Sophist (as we have remarked on Menelaus doing at 497-99!) should declare with conviction of his sighting of 'Helen' at Troy, 'and the mind sees!'

7. On this Sophistic contrast in *Helen*, see F. Solmsen, '*Onoma* and *Pragma* in Euripides' *Helen*', *CR* 48 (1934), pp. 119-21. Cf. also John Griffith, 'Some Thoughts on *Helena*', *JHS* 73 (1953), pp. 36-41.

8. Cf., in this connection, Dale's note on 16ff., where she finds Helen's scepticism 'curious and not a little upsetting'. Surely not in Euripides, and certainly not in *this* play!

9. The text of 1050ff. has been doubted, wrongly I think, as 'unattractive': see Dale's note *ad loc.* and references there given.

10. A.S. Way, *Euripides, with an English translation* I (London and New York, 1920), by adding 'it seemeth' to his translation of 1119-20, and, more surprisingly, A.M. Dale, in her note to 1104-64, take this reference to Helen to be a reference to the *phantom*, not to the real Helen. But there is nothing in the Greek to suggest this.

VI. Nomos and Related Ideas

1. Guthrie (1971), pp. 56-7. (Guthrie's whole discussion of 'the *nomos – phusis* antithesis' in his Chapter IV has been most useful in the present discussion.)

2. See above, Chapter I, p. 20.

3. The question of the identity of 'Thrasymachus' in *Republic* I has been much discussed in connection with the two passages cited above (i.e. *Rep.* 336ff. and D-K 85 B8); see the articles by Kerferd and J.P. Maguire reprinted in Classen (1976), pp. 545-63 and 564-90, respectively. In any case, the theory of natural right, whether or not Thrasymachus himself subscribed to it (as Kerferd thinks) was no doubt debated by the Sophists and this is all that is strictly relevant for our purposes.

4. See above, Chapter III, pp. 43-4.

5. Guthrie (1971), pp. 112ff.; for Kerferd's view, also cited above, see Kerferd (1981), pp. 115ff. I do not find convincing Untersteiner's view (Untersteiner [1954], p. 245), that Antiphon's aim is 'the transformation of *nomos* into *phusis* by its reduction here to "universal experience." '

6. So Guthrie argues, particularly with regard to the anonymous writer's defence of law in the interest of preserving community living (Guthrie [1971], p. 72). See also Guthrie's further discussion at pp. 314-15. Cf. also Margaret Reesor in the Introduction to her translation of *Anonymus Iamblichi* in *The Older Sophists*, ed. Rosamund K. Sprague (Columbus 1972), p. 271.

7. Reesor in Sprague (1972), as in n. 6 above.

8. See above, Chapter I, p. 22.

9. David Lupher, *Persuasion and Politics in Euripides* (Stanford University Dissertation, 1979), p. 30.

10. On the somewhat ambiguous expression *diploun kerdos* ('double reward'), which Eurystheus promises at 1043, see Pearson's note *ad loc.* (A.C. Pearson, ed., *Euripides, The Heracleidae* [Cambridge, 1907]).

11. Lupher (1979), p. 27.

12. For the details of Theseus' criticism of Adrastus' disastrous decision, see Conacher (1967), pp. 99ff.

13. On this important point, see C. Collard, *Euripides' Supplices* II (Groningen 1975), in his note to 201-13. I have also found Collard's detailed notes on certain interpretative and textual difficulties in this passage useful in my translation below of *Suppl.* 195-213. On earlier 'evolutionary' accounts, as well as those contemporary with Euripides, see my *Aeschylus, Prometheus Bound, A literary commentary* (Toronto 1980), ch. 4, and references there given, especially to E.R. Dodds, *The Ancient Concept of Progress* (Oxford, 1973) and to Thomas Cole, *The Sources of Greek Anthropology* (A.P.A. monograph, no. 25, 1967). We should also note Heinimann's interesting contrast between Protagoras', Plato's and Euripides' accounts of the evolution of civilized man: Protagoras, from the beginning (Heinimann notes) places man in contrast to animals. (See Felix Heinimann, *Nomos und Phusis* [Basel, 1965], pp. 148-9.)

14. On this and the following point, see Collard's good observations in his notes to *Suppl.* 201-13 and 286-384 (Collard, 1975).

15. Collard (1975) in his note to 308-12a. See also the rest of this good note, as well as his notes to related passages, all of which are relevant to the present discussion. Cf. also Burian (1985), pp. 134-5.

16. E.R. Dodds, on the other hand, in his edition of *Bacchae* (Oxford, 1959), in his note to 201-3, sees 'the glaring anachronism' of Teiresias' reference to ancestral traditions as 'a warning to the audience that the debate which follows will represent a fifth-century controversy transposed into the mythical past'. Cf. also Vincenzo Longo, *A.A.Lig.* 46 (1989), who regards *Bacchae* 201-3 as a palinode on Euripides' part, since he criticizes the Sophists here whereas normally (in this author's view) he regarded himself as one of them.

17. See above, Chapter I, pp. 22-4.

18. Dodds (1959), in his note to *Bacch.* 895-6; his quotation from Anonymus Iamblichi is the passage (D-K 89.6.1) which I have quoted earlier in this section. For a different view of these passages from *Bacchae* and Anon Iambl., see Heinimann (1965), p. 166.

19. See Dodds' note to *Bacch.* 201-3; cf. also D-K 80 C4.

20. Cf. above, Chapter I, p. 28.

21. Karl Deichgräber, 'Die Cadmus-Teiresias Szene in Euripides' *Bakchen*', *Hermes* LXX (1925), pp. 322-49.

Index

www.ingramcontent.com/pod-product-compliance
Lightning Source LLC
Chambersburg PA
CBHW060556100726
47907CB00005B/1385

* 9 7 8 0 7 1 5 6 2 8 1 6 4 *